GET DOWN OR LAY DOWN

A HOOD CLASSIC BY

DERRICK JOHNSON

Street Life
PUBLISHERS

This novel is a work of fiction. Any references to real people, events, establishments, or locales are intended only to give the fiction a sense of reality and authenticity. Other names, characters, and incidents occurring in the work are either the product of the author's imagination or are used fictitiously, as those fictionalized events and incidents that involve real persons. Any character that happens to share the name of a person who is an acquaintance of the author, past or present, is purely coincidental and is in no way intended to be an actual account involving that person.

ISBN 13: 978-0-578-06154-2

Library of Congress Cataloging-in-Publication Data; Johnson, Derrick

Get Down or Lay Down: a novel/by Derrick Johnson

For complete Library of Congress Copyright info visit;

www.streetlifepublisherz.com

P.O. Box 2112

Minneapolis, MN 55402

Cover and interior design by www.MarionDesigns.com

Editing by Sheila Johnson and Kathie Smith

GET DOWN OR LAY DOWN!

This book takes the reader into the heart of the ghetto. It's about how niggas feel about people from other places coming into their cities and hoods, invading turf, taking over and changing their rules of the game; whether it's the fluxation in the narcotics, or how and where they sell their drugs, or more important the way they capture the attention of the hood women.

This tells how one fed up brother, who wouldn't bow down to the outsiders, forms a click of renegade gangsters from various gangs who team up to cause death and destruction to those who have came to their city to rape all the hood's riches and take them home to their cities.

Pleading allegiance to their chief's "cause", none of them fearing anything but their fearless leader, DIG A HOLE, they go on a murder spree filled with a direct message...... GET DOWN OR LAY DOWN!

All praise is due to the Lord God Almighty.

I send my love to my Grandma Eula Belle Johnson. I know you're watching over me and proud of the changes I've made. I love you relentlessly. Thank you for your patience and persistence, especially while I wasn't focused. I now understand what you meant when you said, "Everything is obtainable." I only wish you could have lived to see the first black President Barack Obama. Momma your light still shines on through me.

To my beautiful children Donte, LaShyla, Derrick Jr. and Jewell. Ya'll are why I keep striving!

ACKNWLEDGEMENTS

Much love and respect to all the brothers of the struggle. It's been a long time coming, but now we up in this bitch!

I send a shout out to Snoopy, Galen, KT, Biz, Andy, Montey, Cleatus, Duffy, as well as Lyn (my stepmother). Thanks for taking me in and accepting me as your own; truth be told I don't know where I'd be had you not. My gratitude and respect for you is immeasurable.

To my beautiful mother Vivian, you are truly one of a kind. Even with our ups and downs, I know you are truly irreplaceable. And because of this I wouldn't change one thing because it's taught me to appreciate you and treasure all of our good times together. I love you unconditionally.

Carla you're the greatest. God couldn't have given me a better sister. To my brother Allan, I know we've not seen things eye-to-eye but it's never stopped the unconditional love I have for you. Nothing, including time and space, can change that.

To my aunt Jeweline and cousins Bobby, Chrissy, Dee-Dee and Lamont: although our family is small, the love is tremendous because we're all we got. Uncle Kenny, I'm definitely on my way. To my nieces Brittany and Briana and nephew Torry, I'm very proud to have kin such as ya'll. Uncle Derrick loves ya, always!

To my brother-in-arms Trell, we've seen and done it all: the bond we share is unbreakable. To my nigga DC, what's really good! What up Green Eyes, my Sirconn Gangsta.

Much love to my cousin Terrance, aka Scrilla, at USP Atwater.

Best believe this is just the first of many. The foundation has been laid, the Game has been mastered.....now let's get money!

To all the brothers on lock, keep focused: never take your eyes off the door because it aint over till you breathe your last breath.

To all ya'll out-of-town cats that got us fucked up in Minnesota, thinking it's sweet up here, it's no longer Money$ota, it's Murderapolis.

North Vietnam 4 Life II VI.

Keith from Marion Designs for helping me create this sick cover. Yeah ya clowned with this one, thanks.

Derrick Johnson

PROLOGUE

"Hurry the fuck up man! Close the trunk!"

Quarter Man did as told and kicked the leg of the victim back into the trunk and slammed it shut. It was a cold dark evening in Murderapolis; as cold as a hooker's heart.

As I sit here trying to figure out how the following events took place, I've slowly come to realize that what many of today's rappers rap about was just another average day for a small group of men called the Bogus-D-Siples.

In a state known as The Land of 10,000 Lakes - at least that is the state's slogan - for the pimps, dope boys, and thieves, it was a hustler's paradise. Up north here we don't vibe off of the out-of-towners coming into our city for *any* reason, but the dislike alone didn't stop the flow of people seeking a piece of the pie up here. Consequently, as a result of their being here, a click was formed of local guys from various gangs; those who just didn't seem to fit in with their clicks.

Prior to forming the Bogus-D-Siples, we all hustled crack and the game was lovely. All the local niggas was breaking bread. What we brought in from Chicago we tripled up here. That was until the FBI, and many other out-of-state crews, invaded our turf and under cut the local prices. Due to this, us local niggas decided shit had to be done. This is how BOGUS-D-SIPLES CAME TO BE AND MADE A CITY THAT WAS ONCE CALM INTO WHAT IS NOW KNOWN AS MURDERAPOLIS.

CHAPTER 1

Quarter Man was sitting on the front porch for what seemed like hours waiting on the rest of the crew to arrive for their daily session when from inside of the house Dig a Hole yells for him to open the back door for the guys. Security was a must when it came to the gatherings, solely because they were the outlaws of the city and were notoriously known for laying niggas down and taking whatever, from whomever, they wanted.

At one point every member of the Bogus-D-Siples was once part of an organized gang ranging from GD, Vice Lords, Crips, and Bloods. One particular member of the gangs stood out, one who was different. He was extremely vicious and was always in disagreement with the laws and policies to which the gang was suppose to adhere. Never the one to accept the violations for his actions, he became looked upon as an outcast. Feeling as though the gangs never were originally from his city anyway, he secretly held the desire to rid the city of the outsiders, whom he considered to be leeches that were there to rape his city of its riches and take control of the streets he was raised on.

Patiently waiting for the right time paid off for Dig a Hole. One day after one of the gang's meetings, he saw one of the head members take a huge bag and place it in the back of the trunk of his Mercedes. Not quite sure how the situation was going to play out, he knew this was his opportunity to make his move, and from this point on he was all in. Thinking fast he saw one of the shorty folks; one he knew kept a banger on him and was one of the many who were from Minneapolis who looked up to him and called him Uncle. He involuntarily involved shorty into his plot.

Laying in the cut like a bandaide, Dig a Hole instructed Quarter Man as to the part he was soon to play in the scheme. Patiently they waited on the chief Maurice to come back out of the building. Their wait wasn't long.

Dig a Hole knew that Maurice wouldn't be alarmed by Quarter Man's presence, mainly because at seventeen he weighed a buck twenty soaking wet with the looks of a twelve-year-old. But in his case looks were deceiving. This was a killa; a young cat with no heart or remorse for anything or anyone. He was abandoned at the age of eleven and was adopted by the streets, learning that success of his survival consisted of taking what you want. At eleven he was left at home with an empty refrigerator and a nine shot 22 automatic pistol he stole form one of his mother's many lovers. Filled with total bitterness and the will to survive, he left his home never to return, killing his first of many victims at the age of twelve.

Seeing the gangsta in him, Dig a Hole opened both his arms and houses to the young killer. It was an act of kindness that earned Quarter Man's loyalty for life to the man he now considered his only family.

Upon seeing Quarter Man, coming out Maurice hollered, "What's up Shorty Folks?"

"Shit. Just waiting on my mans to come out," Quarter Man replied.

"Who's that?" Maurice asked, still heading towards his car.

Noticing Maurice not paying any attention to his surroundings, Dig a Hole emerged from the side of the building. Still talking to Quarter Man, Maurice opened his trunk. At this point Quarter Man pulled out the 40 Glock he had concealed in his waistband.

Speaking slowly, he told him to simply "get in the trunk."

Walking up to him, Dig a Hole saw a slight hesitation in Maurice's actions and immediately took control of the situation. He apprehended the pistol and smacked him upside the head saying, "Get the fuck in the trunk bitch."

Hesitating is what cost him his life. Not one to repeat himself, Dig a Hole put one in his head and watched him slump over into the trunk.

Looking back at Quarter Man he shouted, "Hurry up and stuff the rest of the body in the trunk." He almost gave him another dome shot when a nerve made Maurice's leg kick back outside the trunk. Quickly putting it back inside, they hurriedly jumped into the Benz riding off, knowing their actions was going to cause an all out war, one that neither knew how they were going to win, but both were ready and willing to ride or die for their act of Bogusness.

Weeks had passed and no one seemed to know what happened to Maurice. Many had their suspicions due to the fact that the content in the trunk was ten keys of heroin, leaving many of the local dealers drugless. Mysteriously, the powerful drug started to filter back into the streets: only the distributor wasn't the usual one who dispersed the drug. It was Dig a Hole who now controlled the flow of heroin in the city, at least for the time being.

Knowing that he had the only weight in the city he took full advantage and served it raw and damn near uncut. As a result he had every dope fiend north, south and even from St. Paul coming to his spot for their fix. The only way the other dealers were able to cop from him was to pay his prices, and they weren't cheap. In his mind, they deserved to be treated this way because they had no problem paying the out-of-town boys the ticket they charged, so why accept less?

Now having interactions with all the different gangs, Dig a Hole took advantage of the opportunity to watch and observe the various members of the opposing groups, knowing that it would only be a matter of time before everyone put it together that he was responsible for the stolen shipment and Maurice's death.

Recognizing this, he began to assemble his own click to not only distribute his drugs, but to literally take over the whole fucken city. After thoroughly thinking out his plans he set forth the action to make them a reality.

Because he was from Minnesota he was pretty familiar with the other people from various gangs. Already knowing the riders, he started recruiting them individually with the lure of his riches and the chance to do what they wanted, how they wanted, and to whom they wanted.

After several tests he narrowed the group down to eight people ready to chase the fast cash by all means necessary. His team of eight niggas was ready to give the streets of Minneapolis the bizness! This was the start of how eight hood niggas took over an entire city.

CHAPTER 2

One by one they filed into a small house located on the north side of Minneapolis. The last to enter was Dig a Hole. He alone formed and molded the click. The first fifteen minutes of the meeting was bullshit talk of the robbery that they hit last night.

Interrupting the small talk, one of the older members, Zeke said, "Meeting is now in session." That being the cue for Dig a Hole to take the floor.

Addressing the guys he asks, "Is there any news about last night's lick?"

Quarter Man, the youngest in the fold, spoke first saying, "It's going around that we're responsible and word is there's going to be some heat behind this one."

740 interrupted saying, "I told you we should have left them hoe ass niggas stanking." 740 was the gunslinger amongst gunslingers. His motto was simply – "kill them all."

"Quiet down and let's figure out how we're going to pull this next caper off. We'll deal with that other shit when it comes, just keep them thangs cocked," Phat Bogus replied.

"Okay, here's how it's going to go down," Dig a Hole spoke up, once again taking control of the conversation. "I want you to call KeKe. Find out if she still has that mark coming over to her crib as planned. If so, ask her the time schedule."

Ya see, we have one female in the click who does various tasks ranging from recruiting females to knocking potential prey for us. Being how all the niggas feared us, we had to rely on the bitches for intel on the trick ass niggas who came into town.

Now Keyawna, she went by KeKe to the click - she was the ride or die bitch. She had been a part of the team since day one. She was not only gansta, KeKe was sexy. Standing five-feet-eight inches, one-hundred-forty-five pounds, with long, wavy black hair which she kept done, along with her nails and perfectly manicured toes, she stayed in the latest gear. Whether it be Prada or Fendi, she rocked it like it was made for her. At age twenty-four she had seen her share of out-of-town niggas come and go, and to a newcomer coming into our city she was the prize bitch to have (or so they thought).

The crew quieted down so Sinatra could place the call to KeKe. After the third ring a sexy, enticing voice came over the phone. "Hello."

"Yea KeKe, this Sinatra. What's good Lil' Momma?"

"What's cracken my nigga?" replied KeKe.

"Dig this. We're over at the spot going over the plan and was calling to confirm things. So is it still on for tonight? You know we're going for the whole kit tonight baby girl, so don't let him cancel out on ya," Noodle explains.

"Yeah I'm already knowing. I actually just got off the phone with his soft ass and believe me all I had to do was mention to him that this here hot pussy was in need of a good touching up and it was a wrap."

"Okay. What time do we need to be there?"

"Seven. Is Dig a Hole with you?" asked KeKe.

"Yeah he's right here, hold on." Passing the phone, Dig a Hole says, "What it do?"

"Check this out Boo, I have another fish on the line and I believe this is a big one. Check it out. Me and a few of my bitches were out at Club Cristal and there was some niggas from Chicago in there super flossing, buying the bar out and shit. One of the niggas approached me with a bottle of Cristal and you know me, I declined. Telling him I can buy my own drinks, it's the rent I need help with. Like a fish to a hook he took the bait, bragging about what and who he was. Later he was asking me did I have some females who wanted to entertain him and his boys at a private party they were having tonight in St. Paul. I told him I'd see what I could do and took his number down. Real talk, the boy was blinding me with his jewels alone, not to mention the whole crew was iced out. I would have called last night but I knew ya'll was preoccupied with that other matter. Speaking of which how did that go?" KeKe asked.

"All went well and we'll bring your chop over when we come at seven. Look, call them cats and tell them it's all good. Get a few of the girls that are expendable and see what time and where this get-together is. We might just be able to swing through there if all goes well with Steele tonight. Call if something changes. If not, see ya at seven," Dig a Hole instructed and hung up the phone.

"Now back to the point at hand," continuing on as if he never was on the phone, "I'm going to take three of ya with me on this one, but everyone else is on standby for the Chicago cats. Big T, 740 and Fuck U will come with me. Quarter Man, you'll monitor the police scanners from here. Gutter, you'll drive the van to the pick-up spot once we obtain the info. Zeke will go with you as well for security. I want everyone's walkie talkies on Channel 8."

Toot with his stuttering ass asked the dumbest question, "What if you can't get the info out of him?" The cold stare from Dig a

Hole must have been enough of an answer to relieve him of any doubts he may have had.

"Now listen up boys, this is the big one. Hopefully we'll hit him for the fifty thangs he brought in and also be able to make him reveal his connect's location, or set up a buy for us. From what KeKe told me, he counted $200,000 at his spot three days ago. Now, as of yet, we don't know where the money is, but that's only a matter of time. For now let's just lay low until we meet up at KeKe's tonight," Dig a Hole dictated.

Big T was the first to say, "Let's break out the toys" and quickly led the way to the basement where there was enough arsenal to take on a small army. There was everything from 38 Specials to 50 Cal machine guns, Calicos, M16, AK47, and MP5's. You name it and it was there, not to mention the endless supply of ammunition; the deadliest being the black talon, armor piercing bullets. After everyone had their weapon of choice, they all, along with their bulletproof vests, proceeded to leave the spot.

CHAPTER 3

Feeling slightly paranoid, Dig a Hole drove around the block several times before pulling into his driveway. Noticing his boo's car was home he proceeded into the house hoping she didn't go into their bedroom closet and find the fifty grand he left in the grocery bag on the floor. Upon entering the home he was immediately met by the smell of smothered pork chops. Knowing she wasn't one to half step when it came to getting down in the kitchen, he started smiling knowing there were several other dishes to accompany those smothered chops.

Quietly creeping up behind her, he playfully smacked her on her apple-bottom-shaped ass. As she turned around, he started rubbing the huge belly protruding from beneath her DKNY blouse while rubbing gently on his babies and kissing all over her neck knowing this is what she liked him to do.

This being his first child had him overwhelmed with joy because not only was there going to be one, there were two! At times he would allow himself to slip into thoughts of taking the half mil he had stashed and moving down south with his boo and soon to be babies, simply because it would be a safer place for them to raise their children. He visualized living a normal life, being able to ride with his kids and not fear retaliation from something him or one of the guys did.

But hey, that's another life. His reality is "it's Bogus-Motherfucken-D-Siple 'til the world blows up, and this is his city." To leave it would be giving what was his away; something he couldn't imagine doing. So if the bitch niggas wanted his city, or him, they better come with them choppers blazing, because it's a known fact he keeps a banger and it stays cocked and ready for whatever comes his way. It was a hobby sending bitch-made out-of- town niggas back home in pine boxes or plastic bags. Many of the unfortunate ones have yet to be found.

Coming back to his present mind, he asked Candyce, "How long before dinner's ready?"

She replied with a look that told him she wasn't in no rush. Laughing it off he proceeded up to their bedroom to see if his stash had been disturbed. Seeing it hadn't been touched, he moved it to the secret safe he had hidden in the wall. Putting the fifty racks in there, he made sure it was closed and secure and decided to relax and lie down, but not before stripping off his leather Pelle Pelle coat, Sean Jean jeans and sweatshirt, along with the bulletproof vest. He pulled the Mac 11 Submachine Gun from his custom holster, placing it on the dresser, and laid back on his four-poster California king size bed, contemplating the event the night would bring forth and remembering how this particular lick came about.

KeKe had been dating the head of the Detroit boy's click for about four months now, gaining his trust by taking trips with him and assisting him with minor transactions; at times even allowing him to cook the shit up in her house. And now was the time to reap the rewards of her labors. This particular cat was a pillow-talking nigga. After getting comfortable with her he revealed his entire operation. The only thing he left out was the info on his connect. He, like many others, fell for KeKe's pretty hazel eyes, thick thighs and that ass of hers that would put J-Lo to shame. KeKe was the definition of ghetto fabulous. She found out that her trick Steele was giving his workers the night off to go to Auggie's strip bar in downtown Minneapolis, leaving his spot easily accessible to be hit.

Hearing Candyce approaching with a hot plate of that fire

soul food awake him from his deep thoughts and brought him back to his senses. Immediately he grabbed the plate and started to devour the food as Candyce slipped behind him and began rubbing his bald head and shoulders. She threw all her love and passion for Dig a Hole into her massages. She didn't know much of what he did in the streets, but let him know through her touch just how much she worried for his safety and how much she loved him. It was her silent way of telling him "Please come home safe, I can't live without you."

This was a nightly ritual, one that he couldn't resist. No matter what he was doing he made sure to come home for that bomb ass home cooking and love that only Candyce could give him. Sure he had bitches around the hood that he would order to fix meals and prep for his arrival, but that was only to make them feel like they were worth something - he never really ate their food or gave a fuck about them. These bust downs served a purpose, one they would never have seen coming. Candyce had his heart and she had a natural instinct of putting your boy at ease with the touch of her hands.

He knew she loved the gratification it gave her to know that no matter what her man was doing out in the streets he always found the time to come home and allow her to spoil him. It was her way of giving him back the piece of mind that he gave her after her father's death. She was forever indebted and devoted to him for all that he has done. Although he was out most of the day, she cherished every moment she had with him and made him feel like a king when he was home. He knew for the first time in his life Candyce loved him unconditionally for him, not for what he was in the streets, and would never betray him.

Finishing off the plate rather fast, he glanced at the clock noticing it was almost six o'clock. Getting straight up and walking over to the dresser, he grabbed his entire black Dickie outfit with black Air Force Ones and looked over at his Boo.

She asked, "Where are you going?"

Knowing that it would only lead to upsetting her even more, something he tried not to do because of her pregnancy, he headed out the door without answering.

Not one to question him for his actions, Candyce watched Dig a Hole walk out their bedroom door without a word or resistance. As soon as she heard the front door close, a tear fell from her eye and she said a silent prayer to her Savor pegging him to allow her children's father and her world to come home safely.

She couldn't quite explain it but she couldn't help but think that her two little babies inside her started to toss and turn in the same rhythm that her worried heart was rampantly beating. This started to alarm her even more; although she was extremely concerned for her man, she knew she had to calm herself down and relax her babies. If she were ever to lose his two precious babies, she would never be able to live with the disappointment of letting Dig a Hole down knowing that she couldn't control herself and deliver his babies safely into his world.

Candyce shook it off and quickly went downstairs to the kitchen and prepared a soothing cup of tea to help relax herself. When it was ready, she sat at the kitchen table and began rubbing her babies, singing "If You Can't Come, Send One Angel Down" a song her mother used to sing to her when she was a young girl.

Dig a Hole was all she had in this world, her only family. As she sat there singing and rubbing her belly she wished so badly that she had her mother to talk to. Even though he treated her so well and made her feel like she was the most important person on the earth, it was so lonely when he was gone, especially now that she was soon to become a mother.

So many things were running through her mind, she was an only child and didn't have any experience with babies. Not being able to share her feelings, concerns and happiness with her mother weighed heavy on her heart. She found herself more and more lately speaking out loud to her mother, asking her for her advice on motherhood.

Feeling more at ease, Candyce started to clean up the kitchen and decided to call it an early night.

CHAPTER 4

Candyce was Dig a Hole's better half; they met after his brief incarceration in Oak Park Correctional Prison. One day while checking out his trap houses, he saw her. He knew her father from previous encounters, and he knew he was raising her on his own due to her mother's death from a drug overdose. Dig a Hole made passes at her daily to which she resisted.

See, Candyce had a huge dislike for drug dealers. Her mother at one time was a registered nurse working at North Memorial, a local hospital, for fifteen years; her father worked for the City. She never knew how or when their drug usage started, but what she did know is that when she did discover it, it was a lil' too late. They had slowly, but surely, slipped into full-blown dope fiends. Her mother was terminated for missing too much work; and when she was there, she was either scratching or nodding off. Her outward appearance became that of a junkie. With no further options, her Supervisor of ten years gave her an ultimatum: seek help or she would be immediately terminated. She chose to walk away from fifteen years of service.

Her father, Big Jerry, was a strong man. Half Cuban and the other half Black. He seldom spoke and when he did it was barely understandable due to his strong accent. After refusing two on-the-job UA's, he too was unemployed. With both of them jobless, the whole foundation they had built prior to their drug use quickly crumbled.

Little did Candyce know her parents were at one time Dig a Hole's drug testers. When he bought or came up on dope from various robberies, he would give them a small portion to test for him. It was during the time he first jacked Maurice for the ten bricks that he really started using them for his personal genuine pigs, giving Big Jerry a half gram of the uncut dope to see how many times he could cut it. Knowing the dope had to be cut, Big Jerry tried to hide it from Becky. He went to the store to get some Manitol so he could cut the powerful drug, but she couldn't wait; when he returned home he found her on the floor, needle still in her arm.

At that point Big Jerry went somewhere in his mind, never to return; never again speaking another word, thus leaving Candyce to take care of both him and the house. Dig a Hole, seeing her relentless efforts to provide for herself and father by working at Harold's Chicken on West Broadway, would come in and tip her an extra fifty bucks, leaving his cell phone number. Although she never had any intentions on calling him, she accepted his number out of respect and the need to keep him giving her the tips he gave.

One day as Dig a Hole was pulling up to his spot he noticed an ambulance in front of Big Jerry's house. He pulled over after seeing Candyce on her knees crying her heart out and got out to check on her. Quickly he discovered that her father had died in his sleep. Feeling somewhat responsible for the destruction of her family, along with his own personal desire to tap her young pussy, he went over and kneeled down next to her and held her while she cried. He let her cry it out, but shortly after stood them both up and guided her towards his car. After putting her inside he proceeded to take her to his place.

He left her alone for a few days. She stayed there having feelings of uncertainty of what her next moves were going to be, barely eating and at first refusing to talk. Dig a Hole was a patient man, he gave her all the time and space she needed. During this time he went out and bought her a trunk load of designer clothes. Fendi, Donna Karan, Fetish, Yves St. Laurent

- you name it, she had it along with fifty pairs of open-toed shoes due to his foot fetish.

This would be the first time in her life she wore name brand clothes. Still not sure what his intentions were, she remained reluctant to even try them on. Seeing her resistance, he felt it was time to break her in on his intentions. Ya know, lay down his rules.

He started off by saying that the first agenda was to give her father a respectful burial; this he knew would capture her heart and attention. Seeing her lift her sad brown eyes toward him, he noticed a slight smirk.

He then had her attention and continued on saying, "Look, I know that right now you're going through a very difficult time in your life and feel trapped, maybe even cornered. But listen Ma, I'm not here to take advantage of your situation. I just want to show you how good I can be for you. See, I, like you, don't have any family. I lost both of my parents to a car accident at the age of fifteen. As you see, I live in this huge house all by myself. I don't want to put any pressure on you, it's just the opposite. I want to release some of it to make you feel better, loved, appreciated, and respected. This you deserve Ma. Look, all I ask of you for now is to get yourself together. You can have one of the empty rooms upstairs, I'm barely here myself. What I do ask is that you keep some food cooking and have me a plate in the microwave."

Smiling she replied, "When I cook, you better be here to get it hot out the pan." This was the start of their relationship.

After her father's burial she seemed to come out of her shell more as Dig a Hole constantly showering her with an abundance of everything she never imagined was possible. He gave her jewelry, cars and shoes and she got star treatment at all the hottest beauty salons in the city. He had them give her the makeover of a lifetime. When she walked out she was captivating.

Realizing the change in herself, she understood it was partly because of Dig a Hole and his unwavering dedication to making her both happy and understood. It was at this point she made a promise to herself to never allow anything or anyone to come between the only family she had left. She knew that the many men that approached her while she was out and about couldn't and wouldn't make the sacrifice he did, thus earning a permanent spot in her heart forever.

Realizing her growth and the change in her outward appearance, Dig a Hole felt the need to secure his position in her life by impregnating her. Not only was his plan successful, it was more than he anticipated. Candyce became pregnant with twins and with the news that she was indeed pregnant he felt the need to buy a bigger house. She picked out a lovely five bedroom home with three bathrooms and a three-car garage. It had a swimming pool, basketball court, and video game room as well. The area was safe and secure in Edina, Minnesota. A town where the upper class white folks and niggas with money lived.

Despite all the beautiful things he bought her, it never stopped her from wanting him to leave the street life alone. She had such a hatred for drugs, and because he didn't want to keep hearing it, he made the mistake of promising her he'd stop selling drugs - which was seventy five percent true because he basically only robbed people now. After robbing the dealers he would then sell the weight for wholesale out of state; basically recycling the dope because the dealers from out of state only brought it right back.

Knowing that he promised, it was still of little comfort to Candyce. She didn't stress him as much, but nevertheless cried her pretty eyes out every time he left the house, not knowing if he'd return or not, once again leaving her all alone, only this time with two babies.

CHAPTER 5

Walking out the door as fast as he could, he decided to take the black-on-black SS Chevy Impala. Pulling out the drive he realized that in his rush to leave he left his Mac 11 Submachine Gun on his dresser. It didn't really worry him because in his ride he had a hidden stash compartment with two 40 Glocks and a Mac 10. He pulled over and put the car in park. Turning on the emergency brake, air conditioner and the right blinker, out slid a hidden compartment with all the weapons he needed. Putting the two 40's on each side of his waistband and the Mac in his lap, he threw the car back into drive and was ready for whatever.

It sounded like a moving concert inside his whip as he rode

down Highway 394W heading into the city. His music was banging out of control through four, fifteen-inch subwoofers. Firing a blunt of dro and bobbing his head to the Bogus theme song, "Can't Help It But To Be Bogus Man" by Chicago's Crucial Conflict, he remembered to call KeKe.

"Hello" answered KeKe.

"What up baby?"

"Who is this?" KeKe asked.

"Bitch don't play with me," Dig a Hole barked.

"Oh, I'm sorry Daddy. Where you at?" asked KeKe.

"I'm pulling in the garage now. Ya miss me? You know Daddy about to come tax that ass before this shit kicks off."

Smiling KeKe says, "That's what I'm talking about! Come beat this pussy up Daddy."

Coming down the walk, Dig a Hole tells her to open up the door.

What very few people know is that KeKe and Dig a Hole had a secret affair, and the licks they hit was really for their own selfish gain. They merely used the gang as muscle in their endeavors, taking a portion of the proceeds off the top for themselves without the knowledge of the rest of the gang. KeKe was Dig a Hole's first love.

At one time they were the hood's equivalent to Bonnie and Clyde, but all that came to an abrupt end when he caught a robbery charge; one in which his best friend was killed. Her being young and full of cum, not knowing anything but him, she ended up exploring her adventurous side. He wasn't the type to ever forgive one single infidelity and upon release he went his separate way, thus meeting Candyce. Although he has love for Candyce, he can never love another as he did KeKe.

Walking into her house he realized he didn't bring any condoms. He refused to go that route with her knowing how bad KeKe wants to have his first child. Sex is one thing, but bringing a child into the world is another.

Stepping into the living room and seeing KeKe's flawless body lying across the couch with her legs spread wide open and playing with her shaved pussy was cause for an immediate erection. But not one to just enter a house that wasn't his own without first searching it, he quickly searched through the house finding it all good.

He walked over taking his dick out and began waving it in front of her face in a teasing way. She obligingly took it into her mouth, sucking and licking his balls just how he taught her to – from the bottom to the top she licked and sucked. Taking it out of her mouth, he sat on the other end of the couch allowing her to put her perfectly manicured feet on his lap knowing this would turn him all the way on.

Looking at her feet for a few seconds as if to see they were to his liking, he picked one up bringing it to his mouth, slowly flickering his tongue all over her toes, licking the sole from top to bottom, putting all her toes in his mouth at one time while massaging the other foot. Letting go of her foot, she took and slid it all over his face and head, all the while enjoying the sensation of his hot tongue bringing her in anticipation of the hardcore fucking she knew she was about to receive.

Gradually spreading her thick thighs only made him that much hornier, causing him to slowly lick his way on up to her shaved, black pussy flicking his tongue around the outer lips. She started pushing his head down, wanting him to get to the nitty gritty. Resisting, he continued teasing her with a couple more licks, parting her juicy lips and licking all around inside of her sweet tasting pussy while rubbing her clit making her reach an orgasm immediately.

KeKe screamed, "Daddy I'm coming! Oh Daddy get it! Make me come. Suck that pussy Daddy!"

Knowing he had her on the ropes he stuck his finger in her ass, ramming it in and out. Feeling the penetration, she grinded harder against his face releasing all her juices in his mouth. This only turned him on even more, and he commanded her to get on her hands and knees saying, "Face down, ass up!"

He plunged into her asshole knowing she couldn't get pregnant like that. Fucking her with the aggression of a sex god, the tightness of her ass made him cum fast. Sensing he was about to nut, she pushed her ass harder against his rock-hard dick demanding he fuck her harder. Plunging in and out brought forth a flow of hot cum. Taking his dick out and shooting the burning nut all over her ass, she turned around and sucked the nut out his limp dick. Feeling relieved, he laid back on the couch while she went to get a wash towel to clean him up.

After cleaning him off she hopped into the shower to get fresh for Steele.

CHAPTER 6

Knowing it was about a quarter to seven, Dig a Hole called his guys to check on their whereabouts. Recognizing the phone number, Big T answered the call on the first ring to say, "What up my nigga?"

"Shit, just wondering where the fuck ya'll at. It's almost that time," snapped Dig a Hole.

"Shit, we're on your ass like skin. Open the back door my nigga," Big T says.

"Now that's the shit I'm talking about," Dig a Hole thought to himself. He walked to the window smiling, hoping they hadn't parked anywhere close to the house. Not seeing any cars, he proceeded to open the door, greeting each one personally and walking away reminding them to lock the door.

With everyone there Dig a Hole proceeded to go over the plan, but not before yelling to KeKe to bring her slow ass out the room. Normally she would have had a slick comment in response, but hearing the guys out there she knew better than to test him in front of the boys, which would be considered an act of defiance and would result in extreme consequences. He wasn't one to ever be tested or tried; everyone who knew him understood this.

Walking out the room in the shortest of short, pussy cutting Apple Bottom shorts with matching tank top, Manolo heels with her hair pulled back in a pony tail smelling like J Lo perfume, she spoke to everyone saying, "Let's get this money my niggas."

Taking the floor, Dig a Hole started speaking towards KeKe. "Here's the demo. We'll give you a good half hour to work your magic. Make sure you bring him into the bedroom and get him to take a shower. Give him a backrub or a shot of that hot pussy, whatever it takes to get him off guard and disarmed. Once you come out the room to get something to drink, we'll take over. Big T, I want you in the bedroom closet. KeKe, does he search the house?" he asked more out of sarcasm.

With a look like she was just disrespected, she spit out "Fuck no and no other nigga other than you will either." Smiling knowing she was taught well.

He continued on with his instructions. "740 and Fuck U, I want ya'll in the back bedroom. I'll be in the hall closet so I'll be able to hear KeKe when she comes out the room for the water. Now I want this to go as quickly and as quietly as possible. Let's get him gagged, bound and taken into the bathroom where interrogation will take place, understood?" Everyone nodded their heads in agreement. "Now, let's not have any unnecessary shots fired if we can avoid it."

Shortly thereafter, KeKe received the call everyone was waiting on. It was Steele, and he said he was pulling up in front of the house with a homie. Not anticipating him bringing someone else, KeKe decided she'd roll with the plan anyway. Hearing him knocking at the door she said, "Just a minute. Let me put something on. I wasn't expecting you to bring someone with you."

At this point everyone took their spots and waited patiently for their cue. She then went to open the door to let Steele and his guest in.

Steele was looking sexy as always to KeKe. Every time she saw him he made her pussy wet. Although her heart was only for Dig a Hole, she still had her secret desires and he catered to her freaky side. With Steele she got her freak on, but all good things must come to an end.

"Hey baby, what took so long?" Steele asked. "What you hiding niggas in the closet or what?" He asked jokingly. Little did he know if he made an attempt to touch the knob on the closet it would have been the last knob he would ever touch.

Walking into the bedroom, KeKe yelled back out to them to go ahead and turn the game on because she had to slide into something more appropriate.

CHAPTER 7

Sitting in the closet anticipating the next move, 740 sat patiently hearing KeKe move about in the bedroom not knowing when the cue would come, but fully ready to meet any challenges that lurked on the other side of the door.

See, 740, coming from the Southside of Minneapolis, was a part of the growing fad of being a Shotgun Crip. It seemed like ever since the movie "Colors" came out, the Crips, who are predominately on the west coast, niggas seemed to migrate toward the Midwestern states - seeking new territories to invade and bringing huge packages of narcotics of all kinds ready for distribution. They preyed on the smaller cities that had yet to be exploited, seeking out people who showed potential to help and establish their dominance.

They didn't just need hustlers, they were looking for individuals who would carry out orders of violence when need be, and it was at that time 740 stood out up there like a sore thumb. He had a rep for sticking niggas up and peeling nigga's and bitches' caps back, thus making him a prime candidate for their hit squad. After many attempts of trying to get him to do both hustle and be the enforcer, it soon became clear he had one purpose in life – to kill. 740 couldn't handle the stress that came with selling drugs. He'd eventually end up killing all of his customers because he had no tolerance or patience.

During the time Dig a Hole was looking for potential recruits for his Bogus-D-Siple mob, he was hearing a lot about this cat that went by the name 740 who was on the Southside giving bitch niggas the blues and especially cats that were new over there. He was known as a Southsider from anyone in Minneapolis or from out-of-state, that's how he got down. Knowing this was exactly the type of person he wanted on his squad, Dig a Hole set out to find this young recruit. It wasn't hard - all he had to do was go on Franklin and Chicago, the dope strip on the Southside. It was there he ran into 740. He explained to him that he wasn't meant to be a Crip, nor was he meant to sell drugs. He was made to enforce things in his city not just his hood; to put those who weren't deserving of life to bed permanently.

Knowing this is what would capture his attention, he went on to tell 740 he was forming a click of homies who, like him, didn't give a fuck about the daily hustle. His motto was let the hustlers hustle, then go take the fruits of their labor and then he would kill them. Something he loved to do without the pressures of consequences or repercussions from his homies for the heat being brought around.

This was exactly what needed to be said because 740 wholeheartedly embraced the entire concept of Dig a Hole's plan, especially the part of letting him do himself while still getting paid. He went in head first, pledging his loyalty to Dig a Hole's every cause.

Wanting to show his prize bitch off to his boy Corleone, Steele was overly anxious for KeKe to come back out the room without the robe she had thrown on when she came to the door, revealing that hour glass body. Grabbing the remote control and flicking on the huge plasma screen TV, he kicked his legs up to relax and started discussing bizness with Corleone.

Corleone started by informing Steele that with the two hundred bricks he just brought in they would be relocating to Waterloo, Iowa. It was common knowledge that the Detroit boys would go set up shop in different cities, then after stacking a mil ticket they'd relocate to another city or state, just in time for the heat they had caused to cool down.

Hearing all this from the hallway closet Dig a Hole became excited. It was pure luck to run into both the connect and a large shipment of drugs at the same time. See, if the connect was in town that meant that Steele had sold out; so there was both money and a fresh batch of drugs to be gotten. Ready to explode out of that hot ass closet, he remained patient and waited on his cue.

Steele yelled into the other room to KeKe, "What's taking so damn long?"

Replying back with her smart ass mouth she said, "I didn't know I was on a time clock, or that you was bringing someone to my house without letting me know."

Not liking the way she checked him in front of Corleone, Steele quickly replied, "Fuck what you talking about. I take care of your ass, so who and when I bring someone over here is my bizness."

KeKe was smiling behind the bedroom door the whole time thinking, "Bitch ass nigga keep that attitude because in twenty minutes we'll all see who does the barking around this bitch," but for now she'd let him get his role out. At the same time she'd play hers out to the fullest. She walked out the room and was all smiles, bringing along a blunt of dro to further relax them. Handing it to Steele he leaned back to admire her juicy, thick thighs in those pussy cutting shorts, assuming she was rocking them for him.

Still gazing at her backside, Steele says to KeKe, "Baby why don't you hook me and my mans something up to eat. He just came in from a long trip and could use some of that fire shit you be throwing down for me."

"Sure, anything for you Daddy," she replied, soothing his overinflated ego. Turning around she walked toward the kitchen knowing both sets of eyes were following her ass as it shook from side to side naturally. Being that the bedroom was closer to the living room, she went into the bedroom first to let 740 know to come out. She told him she was going to let Dig a Hole out as well, telling him now to post up by the door just in case. She then proceeded down to the hallway closet to let Dig a Hole know it was time to get down.

Coming out with the speed and agility of a leopard, he was down the hallway and in the living room literally in seconds standing over his prey. Not giving them a chance to realize what was going on he smacked Steele upside the head with the 40 Glock. The sound of Steele's flesh meeting his gun was enough to wake Corleone up out his sleep only to be knocked out cold with 740's Mac 11. It was then Big T emerged from the backroom.

Not sure what was going to happen next and thinking it was a petty robbery, Corleone held out his Cartier watch without saying a single word. Big T punched him in the face knocking him on the floor. Standing over him, gun in hand, Dig a Hole went to work duct taping him up hog style.

Judging from the fear in Steele's eyes, it was clear he now understood this wasn't a by-chance robbery. Scared to speak with two guns being pointed at his dome, he chose to play it by ear, while making a silent vow to remember all the faces of these niggas because they were definitely going to pay for this with their lives.

Big T was the first to break the silence by telling him to place his hands on top of his head and to roll onto the floor. Also instructing him to lay flat on his belly, making it clearly understood that any false moves and he would meet his Maker. Seeing nothing but death in his coal black eyes, Steele thought it would be in his best interest to comply, just hoping they didn't discover the Glock Nine hidden in the small of his back. His hesitation cost him being smacked once again upside his head, rendering him unconscious.

Coming to in what seemed like hours, but was merely minutes; he was bound, gagged and naked as the day he was born. Steele could only open one eye, the other was swollen shut, and tried looking around to see if he could find Corleone but couldn't. He then tried to figure out where he was. It only took him a few seconds to realize he was on the floor in KeKe's bedroom. He thought it would be in his best interest to not let anyone know he was back conscious, thinking he might be able to at least hear what their intentions were, but the sound of a wounded and desperate man squealing brought him to the realization that things would only get worse.

Straining to hear what was being said in the other room was hindered by the increasing pounding from the headache that seemed to be explosive. From what he could hear, he could tell that Corleone was being interrogated and viciously tortured. After seeing KeKe pass through the room with what seemed like a frying pan, he closed his eyes and said a silent prayer.

CHAPTER 8

"Now I'm only going to repeat myself one more time," Fuck U screamed in Corleone's ravaged face.

It takes a hell of a man to stand the type of torture Corleone was being subjected to, but after one realizes that no matter what he says he isn't going to live, he'd rather go out like a soldier. What he didn't know is death would have been a pleasant retreat compared to what was in store for him if he continued to not cooperate, because of his current position he was in bad shape. He laid asshole naked, legs spread apart as hot fish grease was being slowly poured onto his exposed genitals, making his eyes roll back in his head along with white foam seeping out the sides of his duct-taped mouth.

KeKe spoke up saying, "He's ready to talk now. Take the tape off him."

Dig a Hole had other plans saying, "Leave him in this tub to marinate for a while. Let's see if his buddy will make better choices."

With that being said, everyone piled into the bedroom but was stopped short by the sudden burst of laughter from 740. Laughing he said, "This pussy done passed out again. I told ya'll these niggas from the 'D' didn't have any balls."

This brought laughter from everyone except Dig a Hole; he was all bizness right now. Dead serious he said, "Get this hoe ass nigga up."

They snatched Steele up off the ground and strapped his naked ass to a wooden chair brought from out the kitchen. Dig a Hole didn't say one single word during the process, but once Steele was secured he knelt down in front of him. Steele looked up at Dig a Hole's dark face and even more dark and devious eyes that said he didn't give a fuck about the next man's life - seeing a stare that would make Lucifer himself shit bricks. As Dig a Hole's stare lingered, the vulnerable man sitting in front of him began to shutter as he sat there helplessly bound and gagged, not knowing what would happen next.

After several seconds of the stare down, Dig a Hole broke

the silence by saying, "Look, I've spent the last twenty minutes dismantling your boy. His balls are gone, he has no fingers on his left hand, and he's missing his right ear, not to mention a few other things. I'm tired of the fucken games and I promise you this, neither of ya'll will leave here tonight, nor ever. But what I will do is this, unlike your faggot ass boy, you can go to hell without the agonizing suffering he's been through and I aint even done with his ass yet. See, I hate and despise all you 'D' boys coming into my city, hustling my streets and disrespecting the game."

Leaning closer, and in a voice only audible to Steele he says, "No one fucks my bitch and lives to tell it. So you can and will get it one hundred times worse than your homeboy in the other room."

He pulled back to see if he was making himself clear. The only thing that was clear was the look in Steele's eyes; the look that let him know he was not only scared, he was terrified. Steele had tears streaming down his face, all the while shaking his head and mumbling something incoherently while looking at KeKe.

"Shit, aint no sense looking at me Trick Willie! Mr. Big Baller, Shot Caller. You pay the bills, remember? Ha, ha. Who's the man now, hoe ass nigga?" KeKe taunted and then walked up to spit in his face before leaving the room.

"Now look, I'm going to ask you one time, and I mean

one time only, where the money and the dope is. And let me tell you, if I even assume you're holding out...." Stopping in mid-sentence as if to find his next words, he looked over to Big T and said "Go get Meathead out of the basement. I haven't fed him in two days."

Hearing this, Steele's eyes rolled into the back of his head. He had a great fear for KeKe's dog. Meathead was a red nose pitbull that weighed ninety pounds. This was a huge pit: he put the "V" in vicious. Shaking his head trying to signal with his eyes that he understood, his efforts were useless because no one paid any attention to him: Dig a Hole had a point to make.

Upon hearing Big T in the other room getting Meathead riled up brought extreme terror to Steele's eyes. Meathead emerged through the door tugging and pulling on his leash and foaming at the mouth as Dig a Hole took his leash, bending down to physically restrain him. He looked at Steele one last time before saying, "I want every piece of dope you know of and money as well. Do I make myself clear?" Without waiting for a gesture or response he let go of Meathead.

Attacking with such a ferocious and brutal assault, Meathead went straight for the kill, first tearing a portion of his jaw off. He continued to bite any exposed body parts after Steele fell over in his chair. It wasn't long before the scene was a bloody mess.

Stopping him before he killed Steele, all Dig a Hole had to

say was "Done deal" and on command Meathead stopped the assault and went to post up next to his true master. Standing over Steele's trembling body, observing the damage done, Dig a Hole told KeKe to bring a jug of cold water. Pouring the water on Steele to see the real damage done he noticed a huge chunk of his nose was tore off, along with part of his jaw. Throwing more water and a towel to his face brought Steele out of his state of shock.

Looking around Steele suddenly realized that it wasn't a nightmare after all, that he was really looking into the face of Lucifer himself. With the tape tore half off from Meathead's attack he readily volunteered all the info he knew. He had thirty bricks on the Southside of Minneapolis that were being guarded by two juvenile males. He also snitched that Corleone had an additional two hundred and fifty bricks and $300,000 in cash at the Marriott downtown.

Leaving out the room, Dig a Hole's last remarks to him were, "For your sake, you better hope it's all there."

CHAPTER 9

Picking up his walkie talkie, Dig a Hole gave out the address and instructions to Gutter, Zeke and Toot who were waiting on standby in the van. After all was said and done his last comment was, "Be safe and bring it home."

Turning to KeKe and Big T he then proceeded to give them the instructions of the next part of his plan. He told KeKe to check on her dresser for the keys to the hotel, they had laid all the contents of their victims' pockets on the dresser. After coming back with the keys he then told her that she was to go to the hotel to retrieve the rest of the dope.

Pulling KeKe to the side, Dig a Hole discreetly told her to put up fifty of the bricks and a hundred stacks of the money as well, and that she was to rent a room prior to going up and getting the package. As soon as she got to the room she was to then go get the package and put up the bricks and stacks, bringing the rest back saying there was only two hundred of cash and work. KeKe gave him the look letting him know she fully understood what he was asking, or rather telling, her to do. Locking the door after her and Big T left out, Dig a Hole, Fuck U and 740 sat back to watch the last quarter of the basketball game.

CHAPTER 10

"Listen up!" Dig a Hole said, "It's a go."

"There's a spot over south with at least thirty of them thangs in it. It's on 27th and Blaisdell and there's only two shorties in it. Now here's what I think." Zeke paused before going on. "I think we should do the narco lick, being how they're shorties, they won't ride out when we hit the door. More than likely they'll throw them if they got any and by the time they realize what's really going on we'll be all over their asses like skin, ya feel me?"

Gutter looked out the side window of the van. Still contemplating which entry would be best, he broke the silence by simply saying, "We'll see when we get there."

The squad pulled up shortly at the location and parked a half block away so they could still see the house. It appeared to be empty or abandoned from the first pass through, so they decided to drive by it again. None of them could tell the status of inside the house so it was agreed upon by all three that the narc move would be the best entry.

"Load'em up! Let's get these fuck boys," Zeke said.

The only sound that could be heard throughout the van was hollow-tip bullets being loaded into their chambers. Exiting the van and jogging in stealth mode allowed them to reach their destination in seconds. Upon walking onto the porch they all pulled out their firearms while easing on the porch. Toot opened up the screen door and Zeke held up three fingers. Seeing everyone understood, he silently counted off "1.. 2.. 3." By the time he reached three he was yelling "Search Warrant! Minneapolis Police!"

He kicked the door lightly, not intending for it to fall in. This was part of the technique to give the occupants time to throw anything they may have, believing the police were raiding them.

Not even two seconds later the door came crashing in and in came the three goons running in full force, ready to kill anything that moved. Like a Special Forces Team the three of them ran through the unit. One went straight to the living room, and just as assumed there were three lil' niggas lying on the ground looking like deer caught in headlights.

Toot remained in the living room while Zeke continued running straight up the stairs with Gutter running throughout the rest of the lower house. After hearing both yell, "Secure," they proceeded to tape up the shorties.

Being the first to speak after the tapping was done, Toot said, "I thought there were only two people supposed to be here?"

"What's the fucken difference? Go look upstairs for the dope before I tape your ass up," Gutter said.

Toot, knowing Gutter had a severe dislike for him, did as he was told and went upstairs. Within three minutes of entering the house they had secured the perimeter, bound the occupants and were now in search mode. Zeke, being the most devious of the three, put his 40 Glock in what appeared to be the youngest one's mouth and said, "Where's the dope Playboy?"

Without hesitation the kid said, "Under the couch."

Lifting the couch in plain view he saw it all just like Dig a Hole said it would be. He immediately called the rest of the team back into the living room and told Toot to pack the shit up, because at this point he and Gutter had mischievous, almost sinister, smiles on their faces. Looking at him, Gutter asked, "How you want to do this?"

"Slow death," was Zeke's only reply. He enjoyed killing, but even more, he loved doing it in a way where his victims died slow deaths. No more needed to be said. They pulled down the pants of the three victims and cut their dicks and balls off, leaving them to bleed to death while bound up hog style.

"Damn it," Toot grunted, upset that he got blood all over his custom Jordans. He walked over to one of the closest victims while they were all squirming about on the floor clearly in pain and kicked him ruthlessly in the face several times before leaving to catch up with the guys.

CHAPTER 11

Pulling into the parking ramp at the Marriott, KeKe wasn't sure if Big T would attempt to come in with her. She also wasn't sure if the room Corleone had was empty and didn't know if it would be a good idea to bring him along. But being one to trust and follow Dig a Hole's leadership, she went with the flow by first checking her Chanel purse to make sure her Nine Millimeter was there. Feeling the cold metal gave her the sense of security she was looking for.

Thinking quickly she looked over to Big T and said, "We probably shouldn't go in this parking ramp due to the surveillance cameras. Why don't you go back out and circle the block a few times; I'll hit you up as soon as I'm on the way down."

Without a second thought he agreed. His only concern was her safety because it would be hell to pay the piper if something happened to her. Besides, quiet as kept, he had a secret crush on KeKe. One time he came real close to fucking her sexy brains out when she was drunk.

Walking to the door casually in her sexy walk, she entered the lobby of the hotel. Seeing the check-in desk she made her way over to it. Upon reaching the counter she pulled out the fake i.d. she had along with her prepaid Visa, knowing the hotels downtown wouldn't accept cash. She was greeted at the counter by a red-faced, older man with short hair in the beginning stages of balding. The clerk asked, "May I help you?"

In her sexiest voice she said, "I'd like a single for three nights please." Noticing he couldn't stop from staring at her cleavage, she leaned over farther to give him a better view. After she filled out the registration form, sliding the form back he processed her room without even asking for her i.d.

With key in hand she made her way to the nearest set of elevators and pushed the button to the seventeenth floor. Getting off the elevator she saw a house phone in the hallway. Picking it up she called the room Corleone was renting, Room 1734. Seeing there was no answer, she walked to the room, inserted the plastic card and, with pistol in hand, she cautiously entered the room. After quickly checking the whole suite, she saw that she was alone and that the room hadn't been used. Dig a Hole had taught her to be meticulous in everything she did. Looking around she noticed that his suitcases were sitting neatly in a closet.

After feeling satisfied that there wasn't anything else hidden she proceeded to go through the luggage, leaving everything in the room except the drugs and money. Knowing it would take her multiple trips to carry all the dope, she quickly exited as fast as she came in, getting back on the elevator, only this time going up again and exiting after two floors. She went to the suite she rented herself. Upon entering she went to the bedroom and took the bricks out the bag, along with the one hundred racks that she carefully hid behind the dresser. After feeling secure it was all hidden, she then radioed down to Big T informing him all was well and she needed him to help her with the remaining suitcases.

CHAPTER *12*

"What the fuck is that smell?" 740 said more to himself than to anyone else.

"Who knows?" said Fuck U after sniffing the air.

It was at that moment Quarter Man came in on the walkie talkie asking did anyone hear him.

Seconds later Dig a Hole picked up and said, "Talk to me."

In response he heard Quarter Man say that the kids are back from daycare and that they brought home their bag lunches, also Momma just called and said everything went well at the salon and she would be home shortly.

"Good. Tell Momma I said put her seatbelt on and drive

safely. Also, tell the kids to stay put until pops gets there. I'm out."

Hearing everything went well, 740 looked at Fuck U and Dig a Hole with that smile he always displayed before he got to do him. Smiling he said, "Let's do this." Knowing exactly what he meant, Fuck U followed him into the bedroom while Dig a Hole went to get Meathead who was whining and scratching at the door. Deciding to deal with Corleone first they went to the bathroom. After looking at his stiff body and checking his pulse, they knew his ass was like the civil war: history.

"Damn," Fuck U said. "I wasn't done with that pussy motherfucker either. Especially after trying to play hard."

Hearing Meathead coming through the house, they both laughed at Dig a Hole's devious ass. Suddenly they heard Tupac's "I Hittem Up" coming through the speakers that were all over the house. Knowing what was next, they watched as Meathead emerged from behind the door, rushing into the bedroom, growling and foaming at the mouth, his eyes locked on his prey. He relentlessly attacked Steele, biting and locking onto whatever body part he grabbed. He shook it viciously tearing huge chunks of meat from his defenseless victim, while Dig a Hole camcorded the entire show. Ripping his throat out with the slightest of ease, Meathead continued to mangle Steele for the next twenty minutes. Feeling enough was enough, Dig a Hole called Meathead off and put him back in the basement to cool off.

Looking around the room at all the flesh and blood seemed to excite 740, but hearing Dig a Hole's voice brought him out of his trance. "Check this out right. Now we don't have to worry about cleaning up all this because we're taking the body to the farm. Let's get down on this Playstation 3 - that's if ya got some of that money to lose." Smiling, they all sat back as if they didn't just commit two gruesome murders. Waiting patiently for the call from KeKe, they played Madden '09.

Soon the walkie talkie came alive with KeKe saying, "Hey baby boy let me in."

He checked out the window before going to the door and felt satisfied that all was well and opened the door. The first thing he saw was Big T carrying what appeared to be two Kenneth Cole suitcases up the stairway. "Leave them in the car, we won't be here long."

Looking at KeKe he said, "Get anything of value and be ready to roll in twenty minutes. We're torching the place, so aint no coming back." KeKe being the soldier she was went about her bizness, but not before giving him the signal that she did in fact handle the bizness as he instructed her to. Smiling back to acknowledge she did a good job, he too then proceeded to clear the house out.

CHAPTER 13

With everyone accounted for, Dig a Hole went about counting the take from all the licks they just hit. With a total of two hundred and thirty kilos and two hundred stacks cash, it was time to discuss distributing them. Everyone agreed it was best to ship it all out of town to their connect on the Westside of Chicago to a close acquaintance of Dig a Hole's; a guy who went simply by the name of Lord. Lord was a person Dig a Hole met during his incarceration, someone he took a liking to. Considering his dislike for out-of-towners, he had abundance of respect for Lord. They at many times discussed the bizness relationship they would like to have upon release, even at times discussing intimate details about their women, KeKe and Dominique.

See, what they both had in common was a foot fetish for bitches with pretty feet, and both their girls had them. Trading pictures of each other's girl at night lead to the two of them liking each others' bitches. Being the players they were, they didn't hide their desires - they did just the opposite. They told each other about it and agreed that they'd let the other fuck the other's bitch, especially after discovering that both of their girls had a sweet tooth for pussy. So from time-to-time when going to meet to do bizness, and after all was taken care of, he'd allow Dig a Hole to fuck his girl and KeKe, or vice versa. Sort of perks from doing bizness, so to say. Any way you want to put it, it was a freak show.

Splitting the cash up with everyone taking about 16.5 a piece, KeKe proceeded to make the call to Carmen letting her know they'd be coming through. "So money up, because this was a big load, especially if all went well with the niggas in St. Paul."

After the brief call, she asked Dig a Hole should she call the niggas she met in the strip club. Giving her the okay, she called them. Dialing the number, all attention was on KeKe. With the success of the previous lick, everyone sat thinking of what their money was going to be spent on.

"Hello. Can I speak with Stoney?" KeKe said into the phone.

"Who's calling?" inquired the man on the other end.

"Destiny. I met you at Club Cristal the other night."

"Oh yeah, Lil' Momma with the huge ass." Smiling as he recalled her sexy ass.

"Anyway, do you still need some girls for the party, or are you straight?"

"Most definitely Lil' Momma. But dig this here...we don't want no shy or scary hoes. We want some bitches that want to get down for their crown, ya feel me? This party is strictly hood rich niggas. We don't want no bitches that aint willing to bust down for this paper, ya dig?"

"Yea, I dig and so do my bitches as long as ya'll drop those chips out ya hood rich pockets."

"That's what I'm talking about baby - cash money."

"So what's the address and the time ya'll going to be ready for us to roll through?" After getting all the necessary info, she finished the conversation by saying, "Look here baby boy, you save your dollas because I got a special surprise just for you. I'll show you how a real bitch gets down for cash money!" Laughing she got off the phone thinking to herself, "If he only knew."

Getting off the phone KeKe looked at Dig a Hole to see if she could continue with the info, or did he want her to tell him first.

Seeing that he nodded his head to carry on, she spoke up

saying, "Here's the demo. The party's in St. Paul on the eastside. The address is 196 Afton Drive. The cat's name is Stoney. He said to bring at least five bitches and to come ready to get down. So from my feel of these niggas, they wanting to trick off tonight and stunt showing off. When I met them at the club they all had on enough ice to cause a snow storm. My guess is tonight will be no different."

KeKe had a father in Denver who fenced all our hot jewelry. He'd separate all the ice from the jewels then melt all the gold down into untraceable bars.

Posted up in the back of the room listening, at the same time in his head going over every probability as well as preparing for the improbable, looking up he gathered his thoughts and took charge like the Chief he was. Dig a Hole said, "Listen up! KeKe, you take care of assembling the hoes for the show. Make sure they're expendable; don't tell them anything as far as location goes. Just that it's a bachelor party. We don't need them letting anyone - outside of who's going - to know about their one-way trip. I want 740 and Fuck U to come with me. Everyone else will meet back up at twelve o'clock – stay in the shadows."

Walking off he tells KeKe, "Come here. Look baby, I want you to go to the room and get the work and cash out of there. I'll meet up with you later." See, after hearing she left Corleone's luggage with his clothes and stuff in the room, Dig a Hole didn't want to leave any strings untied to draw suspicion. A dead man can't retrieve his luggage, and not knowing if he had anything in it to identify him, it just simply wasn't worth the risk. After telling her where to put the shit up, he, 740 and Fuck U took the Chevy G20 conversion van and left.

"Where we going, Dig a Hole?" 740 asked from the rear of the van.

"Head over to KeKe's. It's now dark enough to bring those bodies up out of there, ya dig?"

"Fo sho my nigga. We taking them to the pit?" asked 740.

"You already know. I'm sure there's more than enough lye left in the barn to handle them two pussies."

After wrapping the stiff bodies in plastic and loading them into the van, everyone put their seatbelts on and headed out to the abandoned farm that Dig a Hole had purchased from an auction a few years back. It was thirty minutes outside the city, a perfect place for doing things like they were on their way to do.

Pulling into the barn and leaving the headlights on, the three of them hurriedly took the bodies out the van to a shallow pit less than a quarter mile away from the barn. Running back for the lye, Fuck U returned with both the lye and a flashlight. Being it was so dark they needed to make sure to cover the entire face, hands and feet with it; the whole body if possible. The lye was worse than battery acid. Within twenty-four hours the flesh would dissolve and the lye would continue to eat at the bones of the skeletal remains.

Because of Dig a Hole and his crew, the field that they were standing in was filled with casualties of the Bogus-D-Siples. Seeing that the latest bodies were properly disposed of, Dig a Hole grabbed the plastic the corpses were wrapped in and started heading back toward the barn. Stopping to light a square, he looked back only to see Fuck U and 740 pissing on the bodies of the niggas they just dumped. Laughing, he said, "Goon squad to the end."

After putting the plastic in the van, he backed it out the barn, closing and locking the doors afterwards. Heading back toward the city, Dig a Hole instructed 740 to slide past the place the Chi-Town cats were throwing the party so he could check out the area. He then told him to ride over the bridge going into St. Paul so he could get rid of the plastic in the river. Sitting in the back smiling, Fuck U didn't say a word as he just looked at Dig a Hole with total respect and admiration for being so methodical and careful, never leaving a loose end.

After checking out the area and mapping out possible escape routes, they headed back toward their side of town, the North Side.

CHAPTER 14

"Girl look, these niggas is the cream of the crop. We all should leave up out that bitch paid tonight. I told him it was three hundred dollars just for us to walk through the door." Although KeKe didn't discuss this with Stoney, she only wanted to say whatever it took to get the girls to the party; she'd work the rest out later.

Feeling his phone vibrate, Dig a Hole answered it saying, "What up?"

In her sexiest voice KeKe said, "Nothing Daddy. I've handled all that, and am patiently waiting on your call Daddy."

"Everyone ready to move?" he asked.

"Yea Daddy. Just as you said, five of them hoes and they're all expendable as you asked. But before we go, can you come scratch my itch? My pussy's on fire and I need you to come put it out. Please Daddy!" she said, more begging than asking.

"Where you at?"

"My sister's."

"Damn Boo. You know I hate coming to that damn house." He said irritated.

"She's not here. She's at church doing one of her bible study classes."

"Should of knew." He snorted.

See, it was known by very few that KeKe had a twin sister named Keyawsha. They were identical; even as adults it was hard to distinguish one from the other. Looks was the only thing they had in common, they were as different as day is from night. Keyawsha was a preacher of her own church, and KeKe, well, she was Bogus, plain and simple.

Dig a Hole had a dislike for Keyawsha because she would always preach to him about his ways and turning his life over to God. But little did she know he'd already sold his soul to Satan and was trying to figure out a way to con Satan out of his soul, or at least partnership.

"Be there in twenty minutes."

"Okay. You know it's twelve o'clock." Reminding him

because she knew his half hour could turn into three hours.

"Gotcha baby. Warm that pussy up for me. I'm heading there now." Hanging up he told 740 to drop him off at his Impala.

Walking into KeKe's sister's house was like entering a church, pictures and religious shit everywhere. He headed straight to the basement where KeKe had a little room hooked up at. It was where they kept their safe as well. He immediately stripped off his clothes not wasting any time. KeKe laid back watching with a glow in her eyes that said she liked the hard dick in front of her.

She looked good lying on the bed, spread eagle with a dildo up her ass, while playing with her pussy at the same time. Walking over to the bed, he stood there for a few seconds watching the freak show that enticed him even more.

Looking her in the eyes he said, "Bitch get on your knees and suck this dick." Immediately stopping her self-masturbation she grabbed his dick and lifted it up gently jacking it off. Knowing it drove him crazy, she bent down to suck his nut sack and licked from the bottom of his dick back to the head of it. She tasted the precum that leaked from the tip of his big dick and began devouring it, deepthroating it while he grabbed her hair and literally fucked her mouth.

Feeling like he was about to bust, he pulled out her mouth and told her to lie down. Lying on her back he placed her legs on his shoulders and slid his dick in her dripping wet pussy. Not bothering to be gentle, he forcefully rammed his dick into her, trying to knock the lining out of her pussy. Moaning in pure ecstasy, she sucked on his neck.

Pulling back he leaned his head up and started sucking in between her manicured toes, licking the soles and kissing the tops of her toes. Knowing he was about to bust, he pulled out and jacked off all over her feet. Still feeling her orgasm, she continued to rub her clit while satisfied hoping that he may have dripped some cum in her; believing in her mind that this would bring him back to her, forgiving her for how she played him while he was in jail.

CHAPTER 15

"Big T, what it do my nigga? Let me put this bug in your ear." Phat Bogus said.

"Check it out man. This nigga Toot has been acting real shady lately and I can't really pinpoint what he's on, but it aint right." he confesses on the other line.

"What you mean homie?"

"I've noticed how he's been looking at Dig a Hole lately. It's a look of disgust; I see larceny in his eyes man, and just an hour ago he came to me saying he thinks we're getting the short end of the stick, as far as the stick ups go."

"So bring it up when we all get together tonight and if his

bitch ass got a problem, he'll be in the field like the other suckas, ya dig." suggested Big T.

"Yea, I dig." Phat Bogus agreed.

CHAPTER *16*

After a quick shower KeKe was back all bizness, calling the hoes and letting them know she was on her way to get them. Stepping out of the house, Dig a Hole smiled to himself thinking of KeKe and of the what if's and what could or should have been's but quickly dismissed the thought because in his world one only received one chance at showing deceitful ways. And if it they do, if it didn't bring about immediate death, you can bet in time one would be in their future, because he never let shit slide.

Riding back to the spot to meet up with the crew, Dig a Hole was replaying the events that took place that day in his head, searching for flaws or things left unfinished, making a mental note to have Quarter Man start an electrical fire at KeKe's old place, so as to not be suspected of arson. Success was all in the planning. Making his third trip around the block checking out the spot, seeing nothing out of order, he pulled into the back. Chirping Quarter Man before getting out the car saying, "What up my lil' nigga?"

"Shit, just waiting on you," he replied.

"Well wait no more. Open up the back door."

Walking into the spot and seeing everyone had their game faces on brought reassurance in his mind, letting him know that everyone was taking this seriously and not taking anything for granted; especially when going on licks where they had to freestyle it with the layout being unfamiliar, as were the victims.

"Okay, check this out. Here's the move - we're going to set a crucial example with this one tonight. It seems our message wasn't being taken seriously. These pussy ass niggas from out of town still is under the impression that this city is still open for the taking. They think we're sweet up here. Well, tonight we commit the biggest mass murder in Minnesota history without firing a single shot. I want examples made and here's how." Dig a Hole paused for a couple of seconds to see if he had everyone's attention. Feeling that he did, he proceeded with is plan.

"I want to give these people a slow death. We're going to shoot all the men up with battery acid and all the hoes will be taped up hog style. We'll then tape their entire faces, suffocating them. I want everyone to wear gloves and every single syringe to be accounted for. We're all going on this one. I want silencers on every banger just in case. Understood?" he asked looking around at his squad.

"Let me get this straight," Sinatra spoke up. "We're going to kill these cats with battery acid and suffocate the bitches, right?"

"Yea." Dig a Hole replied with an attitude that suggested he was surprised by the inquiry.

"Well if I may add something. I'd say let's leave a lil' extra message. Let's strip everyone down naked, bringing the men into a separate room. Then proceed as you've already instructed to give the public an eyeful. Message being that niggas and bitches get the bizness. Fucking with us you'll be found ass out, literally. Ha, ha." Sinatra laughed.

"Sho you right, my nigga." Taking charge again, Dig a Hole looked at Quarter Man and told him to go to the auto store to fetch the battery and to also stop at the Walgreens on Broadway to get a bag of syringes, making sure he sends a bum in there to purchase them, along with ten rolls of duct tape. On the way back to also stop at the Honey Bee to fill the van up while reminding him to make it fast because it was almost showtime.

Sitting back he observed his crew, especially Toot. See, out of all the other members of the crew he had a special bond with him. Toot was Terry's brother and Dig a Hole was as close to Terry as two brothers could be without being blood related. What many didn't understand was that Dig a Hole felt responsible for Toot because Terry was his right-hand man. They went from sleeping in tents together to getting their first piece of ass together. He was killed in a robbery that he and Dig a Hole had committed and, after his death, Dig a Hole made it his bizness to oversee Toot. Seeing how fascinated he was with the street life, it only made sense to be a part of the dream team.

Toot was the only one out of the crew that even knew of KeKe and Dig a Hole's relationship from the numerous times she would come over to his house with Dig a Hole when he was a shorty. He also knew that Dig a Hole did time from the case that he and his deceased brother had committed. Little did Dig a Hole know, Toot was harboring bad feelings in his heart, feeling that it was Dig a Hole's fault his brother was dead.

After sitting back watching Toot repeatedly dial a number, Dig a Hole said, "Damn nigga the bitch is going to be there when you get back. Suit Coat will been done taxed that ass by then." Everyone started laughing because it was a well-known fact that Toot was weak for bitches. He would listen to hoes as though he couldn't think for himself. Had it not been for Dig a Hole he would have been a memory like his brother because the crew was fed up with his pussy-ass ways. Looking up, Toot gave a look that everyone noticed - they knew he had bullshit on his mind.

"Big T," Quarter Man's voice came through on the chirp. "I'm pulling up. Should I leave the van running?"

"Stay in it, we're all on our way out. Let's go my niggas, game time!" was all Big T had to say.

As if on cue, Dig a Hole called KeKe. "What up?"

"Shit. Just shaking and moving baby. It's crunk up in here." She said breathing hard.

"Okay...so how many people up in there? Just give me a number, niggas first."

She began to speak but was interrupted. Speaking to someone in the background, she could be heard telling them to hold on, that she had to take this call. Getting back on the phone once she was in the bathroom she said, "Ten niggas and five females."

Again asking more questions he said, "Have you seen anyone with any burners?"

"No. And I've felt on each and every one of these trick ass niggas too."

"Okay! How the paper looking?" he interrogated.

"Shit, it's on point. Not to mention they came stuntin on the jewels - that's for sure!"

"Okay. Check this out. Unlock the back door and at exactly 2:15 am and do the same to the front," he instructed.

"Gottcha Daddy." KeKe said, taking in his instructions while keeping an eye on the bathroom door to make sure no one was listening.

"Now check this out. Watch yourself because we're coming through that bitch heavy. Do you have a banger with you?" he instinctively asked, although he knew she would have one on her.

"You already know this baby," she assured him.

"Alright then, see ya."

After hanging up, Dig a Hole proceeded to fill everyone in on the plan. "Here's how it's going down. Zeke, Big T, Gutter and Sinatra, I want ya'll to enter through the back door - synchronize all of your watches. Quarter Man, you park around the corner with the van off waiting on our call to scoop us up. 740, Toot, Fuck U, ya'll come with me through the front. Sinatra, make sure you bring the acid and syringes to the back door."

"After the house is secure, we'll send KeKe out back to retrieve them. Now, upon entry at 2:15 am I want the back door team to control the entire back half of the house, and those who come with me will contain the front. Take extreme precautions and cover each others' asses until all the potential threat has been neutralized. Does everyone have their vest on?"

Feeling confident that he covered all the bases, he looked up and told Quarter Man to slow down and make a left in the next alley. Checking his watch and telling everyone to set theirs the same as his, he tells Quarter Man, "Hit the lights and park on the side street." He needed to be quiet and keep his eyes open, making sure Quarter Man parked so that he could see the house's front door. Looking back at his he said, "Let's ride my niggas. Bogus or nothin!"

Jumping out the van like a specially trained SWAT Team and taking their assigned positions, each goon was ready to meet whatever challenge that was on the other side of that door, all knowing this could be their last mission if something went wrong.

Big T passed gas while looking at his watch and started laughing because whenever he started farting that meant death was near. He anxiously looked at his watch again letting everyone know that in one minute it was showtime. On his cue ski masks were pulled down over all their faces.

At exactly 2:15 am as planned, Dig a Hole turned the knob on the front door. Finding it unlocked, he exploded through the door. Catching everyone by surprise, he came running through smacking those within his reach with the Mac 11 as he made his way toward the center of the room. As planned, Phat Bogus held down the entrance to the front door while 740 instructed everyone to lay down, letting those who attempted to retreat to the back door know that they would be met with heavy resistance. Hearing the screams over the loud music assured Dig a Hole that they weren't going anywhere.

One unfortunate stud came rushing out the room, gun in hand, caught a three piece to the dome by Fuck you, he was dead before he hit the floor. Stepping over his corpse, Toot immediately went to secure the room he came out of. Upon entering the room he heard a noise in the closet. Walking over to the door and carefully opened it, he saw what appeared to be a frightened bitch. He dragged her out the closet into the room and realized that this frightened bitch was in fact his girl Courtney, the same one he had been attempting to call before coming on this jack. Shook at seeing her, he made the mistake of saying her name.

Upon hearing his voice she immediately knew who he was behind the black ski mask and yelled, "Toot, is that you?"

"Shut up bitch! Get your ass back in the closet and be the fuck quiet." Heading back out just as Phat Bogus was entering asking was it clear in there. Without looking back he simply replied, "Yeah, it's all good."

In the living room Sinatra was ushering the men into the kitchen after stripping them of their clothes and possessions. He made them crawl on their hands and knees toward the back of the house. Getting irritated from the loud music, KeKe, not knowing how to operate the system, went over and unplugged it. She looked over and caught the mean stare of one of the female strippers. Smiling her devious smile she said, "Get naked hoes. It's a cold game but its fair. Ya'll came to strip, so bitches do ya jobs."

Not one to waste time, Big T walked over the body of the nigga who fell victim to Fuck U and his calico and walked to the nearest female who happened to be a redbone. He violently kicked her straight in the face knocking her teeth out.

Still standing over her, in his deep voice he instructed all the bitches, "Ya'll hoes better be asshole naked in ten seconds or ya'll be lying stiff like ya boy John Doe over there," stressing his point by directing their attention to the dead body a few feet away from them.

Teresa, a half Black, half Philippine bitch, was the first to get naked. She thought to herself that these were some freaky niggas that must be on some fuck shit and that they can have some pussy, but they better believe they ass will pay for it with jail time as soon as it's over. Without further hesitation KeKe instructed all the females to lay flat on their stomachs with their noses touching the floor.

With the swiftness of a track star, she - along with Dig a Hole and Toot - proceeded to tape all their hands up so they would have very little resistance taping the legs and ankles as well. Then they immediately started taping the entire heads, careful not to miss a spot. Realizing they were being smothered, a couple went crazy causing KeKe to pistol whip them unconscious.

Walking into the kitchen, Dig a Hole observed Zeke standing over one of the victims, injecting the battery acid into his neck, as were Big T and Gutter. Within a matter of minutes the only people breathing in that house were Bogus-D-Siples. Dig a Hole chirped Quarter Man to tell him to pull up in the back in five minutes. Looking back he saw Fuck U placing all the possessions in plastic bags, along with the needles and duct tape, while KeKe was giving the house a once-over, making sure no evidence was left that could implicate them.

While looking around she noticed that a female wasn't present. There was only four lying on the floor, when in fact she brought five to the party. Walking into the back room where the John Doe had emerged from, she heard a movement coming from inside the closet. Remembering that Courtney, the chocolate smart-mouth bitch, was in there getting her fuck on earlier, KeKe opened the closet and fired on Courtney who was in the corner with a coat over her head. Walking over to pull the coat back to make sure she was indeed dead, KeKe noticed that Courtney had a cell phone in her hand which now was lying on the floor. Picking it up, she listened in the ear piece and heard a hysterical lady on the other end of the line. KeKe hung the phone up and ran into the other room yelling, "Let's get the fuck out of here. There was a bitch in the closet and she got a call out."

Hearing that they all broke out the rear door just in time: Quarter Man was just pulling up with the lights out. Jumping into the van, screaming for him to get out of there, Quarter Man pulled out the alley cautiously. Sirens could be heard in the distant background as they made their way to the freeway.

Telling him to slow down and not to speed, Dig a Hole sat back, furious on how she got by the search team without being noticed, but now wasn't the time to go into it. Knowing that this fuck up could have cost the team everything, someone would pay for this with their life.

Sitting in the back of the van, Toot silently held his head down while trying to conceal the tears of pain from losing Courtney, the love of his life. Looking at each member of his crew, he made a silent vow to avenge her death some way, some how.

CHAPTER 17

In a remote warehouse in Cleveland, Ohio, a group of men were engaged in a meeting, all having thoughts of confusion while trying to reconstruct the events that led them to have to once again be in the same building together. The men of this group made an agreement seven years ago after completing a training course in narcotics in Chicago: the world would never be rid of drug dealers; it was America's bloodline.

Narcotics had always been around and always would be. So why waste a precious career chasing the low-level dealers when after removing one before nightfall, two more replaced him? Not to mention the twelve-hour days for a measly $32,000 a year when Ray Ray on the corner walks around with that much around his neck and wrist, but isn't old enough to even have a license to drive yet.

They decided it was them who deserved to eat well and ride nice while benefiting from the hard work the dealer made off the unfortunate addictions of others; thus, The Coalition was formed.

The Coalition consisted of eight narcotic officers from different agencies throughout the Midwest; two each from Detroit, Chicago, Ohio and Iowa, working as a secret unit to amass as much money as possible within a ten-year timeframe by taxing the larger drug distributors, at least those who wanted to stay in bizness; sort of like paying taxes to hustle. Best believe if you were getting money in one of The Coalition's cities you'd be receiving a visit, and during that visit a decision would be made to either cut them in or cut it out. Better put, get down or lay down.

For those who complied, they would be allowed to remain hustling, and for those who didn't, The Coalition would take their drugs and money. With the drugs, The Coalition would set up one of their drug dealing boys, sending him off to various cities to move their weight wholesale. All had been going great until one of their main dealers went to Minneapolis and hadn't been heard from since. The last anyone heard was of him meeting with his boy named Steele.

"What the fuck is the problem?" barked Mr. Red. "Is shit so serious of an emergency to bring all of us together?"

Mr. Blue fired back, "Damn right it is! We've no idea where over a million dollars worth of dope is, not to mention our worker. This is a conversation I, for one, refuse to converse about over the phone - even with the code names. Right now we don't know what's what. So every precaution has to be taken until we do know what's up."

"Okay. So what do we know?" asked Mr. Black.

It was now Mr. Green's turn to explain things as he understood them. Speaking loud enough so all could hear he said, "I last seen Corleone two days ago in Detroit. He was instructed to contact me upon his arrival in Minneapolis. He left with the two hundred and fifty bricks. He called me after checking into his room at the Marriott and advised me that he was waiting on his contact person Steele to come pick him up. He said Steele was ready and had the majority of the last batches of money, and that he'd be out the city and back in the 'D' by the following night. Now that's the last I heard from him. His cell phone has been turned off and the same with his contact's phone. I called the hotel he was staying at and according to the cleaning lady his room was untouched; like he never returned to retrieve his things. No drugs were discovered."

"So what the fuck you think? Maybe the punk ran off with our shit," exclaimed Mr. Yellow. "Because if he did, every member of his fucking family will spend the rest of their lives in jail for one reason or another."

"Calm down," now Mr. Green spoke up. "At this point I'm not getting the impression he's went AWOL. Maybe he's been double-crossed. Either way, we need to send someone up there to check into this matter. Any volunteers?"

"Damn straight. We'll go," said Mr. Gray, meaning he and his partner Mr. Brown from Iowa. "Have we retrieved his phone records as of yet?"

"What you think? The last two calls placed from his cell were to the number we have as his contact Steele, and the other is to a 612-239-7540 registered to Keyawna Jackson. The address is 4035 Queen Avenue North.

"Okay, we're on it. We'll go make our rounds, shake a few trees, hit up some of our contacts, and see if we can get a grasp on this situation. But before we go, I know ya'll did a check with the local P.D., but was one run with the FBI?"

"Yea, I have a cousin who works in City Hall who processes all search warrants and she did a lil' snooping and nothing significant came up. At least nothing that would concern us," replied Mr. Gray.

Now Mr. Orange, the methodical one, spoke up; when he

speaks everyone listens. "Look guys this is a very delicate situation, one we need to be very careful of. I have a really bad feeling about this one. Hopefully we'll get our shit back and at that point I think it would be in the best interest of us all to just dump the package in one bulk sale and take a little vacation, so to say; thus alleviating the risk of exposing ourselves and taking these extra risks. Agreed?"

In unison they all said, "Agreed." Before leaving the meeting they all repeated their code to one another, saying it in unison.

CHAPTER 18

"Take us to Duluth, Quarter Man, and stay way below the speed limit," was all that Dig a Hole said during the entire two-and-a-half-hour ride. Upon arrival he questioned KeKe about who searched the bedroom.

"I don't know who all went in there, but what I do know is Toot was one of them," KeKe replied.

After everyone entered the cabin and was seated, Dig a Hole went about deciphering the events that took place; first trying to place every member of the squad in the areas throughout the house. It soon became clear the fuck up was because of Toot's bitch ass, once again leaving him with the side glances of the click because no one understood why he was still breathing after all his repeated fuck ups.

"Now look, here's the deal. What's about to take place is we're going to have to make a move on getting off all this dope and jewelry. So here's how we'll go about doing it - after we all break bread I advise everyone to take a lil' vacation from the city. When this shit hits the press there's going to be so much heat about these mass murders; the heat will come worse than the fire in hell. So Sinatra and Gutter, I want ya'll to take the work down to Chi-Town to the plug. We'll tax him a mil-ticket for the whole shebang. If he has a problem with it, take it over to the Black Gangsters over in the hundreds."

"KeKe, Toot and myself will head to Colorado to cash in on all this hot ass ice. After all that concludes, we'll meet Sinatra and Gutter in Iowa. At that point we'll notify everyone else of where to meet up."

"Now, there's some loose ends that need to be tied up while we're gone, so I need you, Big T and Quarter Man to go over to KeKe's old place and create an electrical fire, starting it from the bedroom. Make sure you grab Meathead and shower the blood from him. By the way KeKe, what do you want to do with your car?"

"Check this out KeKe, my Range Rover is in the shop and won't be out for a couple more weeks. Why don't you let me use yours, at least until you get back," insisted 740.

"Okay, but keep your stank hoes out my shit," she said jokingly.

"Bet that up," 740 joked back.

Taking control of the conversation again, Dig a Hole then said, "Okay. We're making a move out of here first thing in the morning. I want everyone to lay lower than a snail's pussy til I get back. I got a crazy feeling about that bitch in the closet, not knowing who was on the other end of the phone will remain a mystery."

CHAPTER 19

"So this is the place he made the last call to, huh?" questioned Mr. Gray. "Well it looks pretty dark in there, no lights on and no one coming or going. Do you think we should chance it and knock on the door? I'm losing my fucken patience sitting here all fucken night."

"Nah," Mr. Brown replied. "I think we should wait it out. I want to see this place come to life because right now it's dead."

CHAPTER 20

"What the fuck type of people would do this shit? Out of all my twenty-three years on the force, never have I seen a mass murder like this. This here has definitely awakened some people up upstairs. Damn it! We have some sick motherfuckers out on the loose. When we find out who was behind these murders, we'll put them under the fucken penitentiary," growled Sergeant Smith from St. Paul Homicide.

His partner, Sergeant Jackson, quietly continued to go from room to room, carefully observing the victims of the worst massacre in St. Paul history. True enough, he'd seen his share of ugly homicide scenes, but this one really touches home for several reasons. Mainly because all the victims appeared to be African American, and secondly the way the females were killed demonstrated the killer lacks remorse for human life. These definitely were not a spur-of-the-moment murders. He realized that he was dealing with a devious, diabolical person who wanted to leave a definite message. But to whom, he wondered? And exactly what message did the killer want to convey?

Gathering his wits, Sergeant Jackson asked no one in particular, "So, who made the call?" After thirty seconds of no responses, he ordered a police officer to keep everyone out of the house, except authorized detectives. "I want to know who made the call to 911. I want their name and, better yet, I want their asses brought to the station. Not now, but right now!" It was perfectly clear he was emotionally bothered by this particular homicide.

Never in the ten years of being Jackson's partner did Smith see him so enraged about a case. Knowing it wasn't the time for inquisitive questioning, he decided it would be best to at least look interested in the case because, truth be told, he was glad the blacks had killed each other off, because in his racist mind it was population control.

CHAPTER 2.1

Waking up at 5:00 am, Dig a Hole walked through the cabin. Seeing everyone still asleep he took advantage of the quiet and went outside to call Candyce. After several attempts to reach her, he hung up and went back inside to shower.

Walking past all his crew, thoughts of killing them all in their sleep made him smirk because it would be the ultimate deception; him having them rob and kill, and then he robs the robbers and kills the killers – Checkmate. See, life to him was a game of chess. As long as he had control of the board he'd allow the game to go on. But, if he at any time felt himself in jeopardy, he'd do what was necessary to end the game. And right now he had the upper hand, at least for the time being.

Fresh out the shower, he woke KeKe and Toot - telling them in a half hour they was on the road, so eat, shit, do what ya need to – but be ready by 6:00 am. He sat back smoking a blunt, replaying the events of the night before and came to the conclusion that something was going to have to be done about Toot. Although realizing this, it had to wait for now.

"Sinatra, wake up homie. We need to be moving and up out the state so we can make the moves homie. I spoke to the connect in Chicago; he said to come on through, he'll be ready. So it's best you and Gutter go on to the city before it gets too late in the day. Grab the work and be on 94S before noon, ya dig?" Not waiting for an answer, Dig a Hole walked outside. Looking back he tells 740, Quarter Man and Big T to come with him. Once they were all outside, he said, "Look, I have a bad feeling about that bitch in the closet."

"Man, that shit's on Toot," 740 blurred out. "Let me kill his ass Dig. I'm sick of him jeopardizing the crew man!"

"Hold up. He's going to get his, believe me. But right now we have other things that have to be taken care of ASAP. Priority number one, I want KeKe's house burnt to the ground. Do it right and start the fire in the bedroom. Make sure you get Meathead out of there first. It's got to be an electrical fire - we don't need no nosey fire chief asking questions. Secondly, it's imperative ya'll lay low. We don't need anyone to even look our way for a minute, at least until we see how this shit's going to level out. Once we cash-in our merchandise, we're going to relocate to Texas for a while. I trust all of ya'll will follow my instructions to the letter."

"You know we got'cha Dig. Just be careful on the road and we'll hold shit down until ya'll return," replied Quarter Man.

"All right then. Tell KeKe and Toot's bitch ass to come on, and by the way 740, I will let you have him when we get back. Right now he has to drive one of the cars back from Denver. After that, you can massacre his faggot ass." Dig a Hole promised him.

Smiling as though he was just told he could have a mil-ticket, he walked away fantasizing on cutting Toot's body parts into pieces.

CHAPTER 2.2

"No one has come or gone. I don't give a fuck what you have to say, I'm knocking on the door." He walked up to the door and knocked softly at first, then harder after a couple knocks and listened for any sounds. All he heard was a barking dog. Realizing no one was home, he walked back to the van pissed off.

Mr. Gray looked over and asked sarcastically, "Are you satisfied now?"

"Fuck no. My ass is hurting from sitting in this fucken van. My nerves are on edge about this fucken money and my bitch swears I'm off cheating with another woman. So hell no I'm not satisfied," he said as he wiped spit from his mouth from his anger.

Feeling it was probably best to not further the conversation, Mr. Gray picked up his newspaper and pretended to be reading it.

CHAPTER 23

"So Mrs. White, let me get this correct, okay? You received a call from your niece, right?" Sergeant Smith reviewed.

"That's correct."

"And she said there were individuals in the house killing people, right?"

"No! What she said was, and I may of not fully understood her because as I said she was whispering and was hysterical, her words were – "they're dead, they're dead, they're killing everyone.""

"Hold up," interrupted Sergeant Jackson. "Did she say who was killing everyone?"

"She mumbled something about Toot. I couldn't hear anything else after that, except for the noise of the shots being fired; and then some female's voice picking up Courtney's phone."

"Hold on. You said a female picked up your niece's phone?" Jackson examined.

"Yeah. I believe after she was shot because I heard her scream, then the shots followed. Seconds after, a female's voice came on the line and said this bitch was on the phone. She said hello twice and then said whoever was on the phone is dead. Oh, she sounded so serious. I don't know what I am going to do if they find out I'm down here." Mrs. White said with extreme terror on her face.

"Calm down, Mrs. White. We'll do all we can to protect you. If need be we'll place you in a witness protection program," Sergeant Smith tried to reassure her.

Sergeant Jackson sat quietly going over the name Toot. For some reason it rang a bell in his head, and he was making a mental note to run a check on the gang strike task force's files to put a face to the name. Thinking why not use one of his favors, he called Lieutenant Johnson, the commander of the gang unit, and requested a check be run on the name Toot; he asked for it to be done ASAP. After hearing that it was a part of the mass murder in St. Paul, Minnesota's capital, he was more then eager to oblige.

CHAPTER 24

Pulling up in the back of KeKe's house, Quarter Man tossed the keys to her Lexus bubble to 740 after assuring him that he and Big T could handle things. 740 pulled the Lexus out the garage and rode off. Coming out the alley and waiting until he got to the corner before turning on her system so it wouldn't cause undo attention to what was happening at the house. He bumped his favorite song by Cypress Hill, "How I Can Just Kill a Man." Firing up a blunt, he laid the seat back and headed toward Broadway and Washington to get some gas and squares.

"Holy shit, Brown, wake the fuck up! It's the Lexus we're looking for."

"Well what the fuck we still sitting here for?" Brown snapped. Pealing off faster then he anticipated, the van's tires squealed as he floored it to try to get the gold colored Lexus in view.

Hearing tires squealing made the ever-cautious Quarter Man look out the window, only to see a Ford Windstar pulling off. Not sensing any immediate danger, he went back to work on the wiring of the fire in the bedroom.

CHAPTER 25

"Okay look KeKe, I want Toot to drive. His license is valid and we'll lay back here in the back of the van so to not be seen. I put the jewels in the stash compartment. Did you call your Pop yet?" asked Dig a Hole.

"Yeah. He said hit him when we're an hour away from the city and that he has a new jeweler we might want to deal with."

"Cool, good looking baby. Toot, stay on 35W South staying five miles under the speed limit and let me know once we get to Des Moines, okay? Can you handle that?" sneered Dig a Hole with as much sarcasm as he possibly could.

"Yeah, I can," was Toot's reply. At this point he no longer cared about the drugs or money; he was set on getting revenge for the death of Courtney. She was his soon-to-be wife and was three-months pregnant with his kid. He didn't care about why she was at the party half naked. He only thought about Dig a Hole's words, "Kill them all." This alone made him want to see Dig a Hole rot in prison for his evil ways. He was just waiting until they got back, then he'd drop a dime to the homicide unit.

Little did anyone know, he planned on leaving the crew anyway. He knew that there was only one way out – death. He knew too much and also knew all the other members hated him and only accepted him because of Dig a Hole. But in a few days none of it would matter, they'd all be locked away.

CHAPTER 26

While sitting back and going over the notes and listening to the interview of Mrs. White, Sergeant Jackson received a call from Lieutenant Johnson and his instincts paid off. The name Toot came back with a face and he was receiving a picture of his face before he even hung up.

Excited he had a lead, he ran to the fax machine. Looking at the picture, reading the profile and gang status, immediately brought back memories of how he remembered the name. He recalled being brought into a robbery homicide in which one of the robbers got killed. The second one got away but was later charged with the armed robbery. Jackson was the arresting officer and the suspect used the name Willie Roberts, aka Toot. He distinctly remembered this guy because of his sinister laugh after he was apprehended and discovered that the alias he was using was that of the deceased partner's brother.

Seeing that he was a Bogus-D-Siple, he decided to run a check on Galen Davis, aka Dig a Hole. His suspicions were correct. Both were a part of the same ruthless gang that was the focus of a secret indictment by the Feds for racketeering. Anxiously he called his partner Sergeant Smith to tell him to go get a warrant for both Toot and Dig a Hole.

Walking out of his office, Sergeant Jackson was summoned to his captain's office. Fearing what he knew was going to happen, but happy to be able to introduce some new leads in the case, he knocked on the door and was told to come in. Turning the cold brass knob, he entered.

Sitting behind his huge oak desk was Captain Washington, and to the left of him was the Mayor of St. Paul and Mayor of Minneapolis. "Have a seat," the Captain said pointing a finger toward a wooden chair.

Not wanting to initiate the conversation he sat down, looking intimidated waiting on someone to break the silence. The first to speak was Mayor Bradley of St. Paul, "Sergeant, what the hell is going on? It's been two days and you've not arrested a single person. We've got the Governor so far up our asses, he feels like a hemorrhoid. Now what the hell are you doing in the God damn office when we have a pack of lunatic murderers running throughout our city killing innocent people?"

After letting him vent for what seemed like an hour, Sergeant Jackson spoke up addressing all three individuals. "I now have a couple suspects named and identified. I'm currently awaiting search warrants and body warrants for their arrests. As we speak they both have been implicated, and I strongly believe they have their hands in on this one."

"You mean to tell me all you're waiting on is warrants? Give me the goddamn phone. You go arrest them motherfuckers and anyone with them. I'll see to it the search warrants are in order. I want this case wrapped up and over with ASAP, and just maybe if we get convictions on this sooner than later, you'll lose those stripes and get bars. Lieutenant status, ya hear me?"

Knowing full well what he was saying, Jackson excused himself and summoned a squad of detectives to go raid some houses.

CHAPTER 27

Pulling into the Honey Bee gas station, 740 noticed a truck of fine ass bitches rolling up next to him. He rolled down his window and asked the driver, "What it do Mommy?" Turning her head as if disgusted to the fact he would even attempt to holler, he spit a goober into her truck for acting stuck up and parked the Lexus and went to get his blunt wraps.

Being cautious was in his nature due to the fact he was extremely feared. He noticed a van parked in the cut with no one getting in or out; two niggas were inside trying to be inconspicuous. He thought to himself, "It would be their worst mistake to pull it now." Comfortable he had a fully automatic Mac 10, he walked back to the car.

Pulling off Washington onto West Broadway, he kept his eye

in the rear view. Noticing the van still following, he chirped Big T letting him know he was on 26th and Emerson and would be pulling up in forty seconds to meet him outside with something thick.

"Do you think he knows we're tailing him Brown?" asked Gray.

"At this point, who gives a damn? He knows something. With a Lexus like that, he's definitely in the game." As the Lexus pulled over, Brown cocked his Glock 27 and motioned for Gray to slow down.

Pulling in front of the house, 740 emerged from the whip looking back down the way he came. Seeing that the van pulled over, he told Big T to stay put on the porch. Walking into the house with his burner visibly out, he glanced back one more time.

"Who the fuck is them niggas?" Big T asked.

"I don't know, but they been on me since the Honey Bee. They might be the niggas of these punk bitches I spit on up there. Did ya handle that at KeKe's?"

At that exact moment there was a hard pounding on the front door. Instinctively all three of them grabbed their guns and went to the front door. 740 first ran to the basement, coming back up he heard the 44 Quarter Man had getting off, it was rapid fire up in that bitch. Coming through with the M16 assault rifle, he proceeded to spray through the walls and doors.

"Gray you alright?" Brown yelled.

"Fuck! I took one in the side. These sons of bitches were waiting on us." He screamed back.

Crawling off the porch while returning fire, Brown looked up only to see a full fledge squadron of detectives lowering down on the house. Lifting his pistol to fire on them wasn't successful, before he even got it above his waist he was shot numerous times by both the homicide team and Big T, who was on the front porch. Falling to the ground and letting Gray go removed the only shielded protection Brown had.

"We need back up! Get us back up!" Sergeant Jackson screamed into his C.B. "We have three officers down and a full fledge firefight going on."

Realizing they were in a firefight with the law, without discussion the Bogus-D-Siples proceeded to bang it out. Quarter Man took both a gut shot and a bullet through his left eye, collapsing in the doorway. Seeing several more police converging on the house, Big T suddenly understood that this now had become a one-way trip and stood up.

Thinking he was going to take out as many pigs as possible, he raised his MP-5 Submachine Gun spraying bullets in every direction. 740 saw his play and rose with him, only to catch one in his shoulder. Falling to the ground and realizing his gun was empty, he knew it was ride or die. It was only seconds before Big T's huge body collapsed on the porch as well. For about thirty seconds 740 laid still, waiting to see what was to come.

"This is Minneapolis Police! I want any remaining people to come out on your knees, hands behind your head. I repeat, this is your first and only warning," warned Sergeant Smith.

Looking toward his entry team he gave the go ahead to rush the house. Rushing in the back and the front simultaneously, stepping over the bloody corpses on the porch was a costly mistake. Feeling himself go unconscious, 740 opened his eyes. His hand revealed a shrapnel grenade, one of three he brought out the basement. Without hesitation he pulled the pin causing the other two to explode as well, killing thirteen officers along with Sergeant Smith.

CHAPTER 28

Lying in the tub, something she enjoyed doing, Candyce turned the sixty-inch plasma screen on to catch her game shows. Just as Whammy was coming on, her show was interrupted by a breaking news story. Candyce wasn't one to watch the news because it only stressed her when Dig a Hole was out, but her attention was drawn to the screen when she recognized one of his spots. Turning the volume up, she caught the reporter saying that eighteen people died in a deadly shooting, and four critically injured.

Tears immediately began to pour down her face. Dig a Hole hadn't come home the previous night, not that it was abnormal, but what was uncommon was him not calling to check on her. Her body froze and she felt the same feeling within her body with her babies as she did the other night when he left out. She knew know that her children had the same devotion to their father as she did, something was wrong and she couldn't shake it off this time.

She immediately got out of the tub and started looking for her phone. In the process of hurrying she almost slipped from the water pouring out as she moved her huge belly out of the custom designed marble, jet stream tub Dig a Hole had made just for her.

Still searching for the phone she heard from the screen that thirteen officers were killed and five unidentified people were killed in the shootout. Seeing that the phone had been thrown beside the toilet from the water, as she waddled over she prayed it still was functional as she frantically dialed his number hoping she would hear his actual voice and not his voicemail.

Seeing that it was Candyce calling, he tried to sound as calm and collected as possible. He answered on the third ring, thinking she was only calling to inquire about his whereabouts and to ask about why he didn't come home last night. "What's up Mommy?"

Hearing her crying brought instant alarm to him. She never showed signs of weakness and immediately thought of their babies. "What's up baby? Talk to me."

Being so emotionally distraught, Candyce couldn't put

audible words together, so he instructed her to calm down so he could talk to her. This seemed to slow down her rambling long enough for him to hear bits and pieces about the shooting. He promised her that he was okay and wasn't even in town, and that once he got to a landline he would call her. Agreeing, but still crying, she hung up.

Dig a Hole turned to wake KeKe to inform her of what had taken place. Little did he know she was already awake and seething with anger at the sweet and reassuring way she just heard him talk to Candyce, thinking to herself that he once talked to her like that.

Wanting to cry she knew she had nothing else to do but play her position, she so quickly checked herself and opened her eyes. Looking over she asked, "What's up Daddy?"

"Look. Some fuck shit done happened and a bunch of police are dead. We need to get somewhere so we can get the full scoop."

"Baby, we're almost to Denver. With something like that, it will be on CNN."

Realizing she was right, he sat back and tried his best to relax while chirping 740, Quarter Man and Big T only to get no response.

CHAPTER 2.9

Pulling up at the hotel in downtown Chicago, Gutter walked in to get the room while Sinatra called their connect to let him know they had made it. Confirming a meeting time, he hung up and waited patiently for Gutter to return. Seeing him emerge and signaling for him to come in, he grabbed the bags and walked into the hotel going directly up to their suite. Deciding not to call Dig a Hole until after the exchange, they laid back waiting on the connect to arrive with the money.

Pulling into KeKe's Pop's driveway, Dig a Hole anxiously jumped out the car. This was one of several trips he'd made to this very familiar house. Waiting on KeKe, they walked into the house with Toot following behind.

Sitting at an enormous oak table counting money by the stacks was her Pops. KeKe's father was an ex-Black Panther who still kept his underground ties. The majority of firearms Dig a Hole obtained was through Pops' plug. Pops didn't agree necessarily with what Dig a Hole did as far as killing Black on Black, but what he did enjoy was the money that derived from it.

For the custom iced-out chains, rings, bracelets and earrings, he'd give Dig a Hole forty-five cents on the dollar; when he was actually getting more like seventy cents - but hey, in his eyes the young punk needed to pay for fucking his gorgeous daughter.

"Hey Pops. What's going on?" Dig a Hole said entering the room.

"Ole same ole shit, different toilet. So ya'll finally made it huh? I was beginning to think this batch of ice you spoke so highly of melted on its way here."

"Oh Pops, you know we bring all our good shit straight to you!" KeKe said smiling.

"That's right, and as you see Pops will always be ready to take care of ya." Greedily eyeing the bag in Dig a Hole's hand he asked, "Where's the merchandise? Are we here for a family reunion, or to take care of bidness?"

Lifting the bag onto the table, Dig a Hole placed all the

pieces of high-quality jewelry onto the table, bringing a huge smile to Pops' face. Grinning, Pops said, "Now that's what I'm talking about."

He got up to fetch the eyepiece he used to inspect the diamonds. Upon returning, Pops picked up several pieces of jewelry. Letting out a low whistle, he looked over to KeKe and said, "Baby Girl, you got some high-quality stones here. The cut on them is exclusive. Off the top of my head I guesstimate we can easily get $750,000 for this here. I'll have to take them in to get a lil' more thorough exam and to show the boss man. So, ya'll make ya self at home and I'll be back."

Relieved he was leaving, Dig a Hole patiently waited to watch the T.V. so he could find out exactly what the fuck happened. Hearing his doors close on Pops' Cadillac, they immediately turned on the seventy-inch projection screen T.V., turning it to CNN. They saw their spot on 26th and Colfax!

"What the fuck," was all KeKe said seeing her Lexus Coupe being placed on a flatbed. Turning the volume up stopped them from hearing Pops enter back into the house. Standing there wandering why they had his T.V. blasted, he saw the mass murder written across the screen in Minneapolis and immediately put two and two together.

He grabbed his tobacco pipe, the reason he came back in, and turned around to leave, catching Dig a Hole's attention. Neither saying anything, due to both being in their own thoughts.

Focusing attention back to the T.V. the reporter announced, "The bodies of thirteen homicide officers are being pieced back together due to the explosion; some of those who were closer to the blast have parts missing. The three individuals on the porch aren't recognizable, but two who were near the sidewalk were killed by either bullets from the homicide officers or the suspects on the porch. They have been identified as Tyrone Davis and Demareo Williams, both narcotics officers from Des Moines, Iowa. No explanation has yet been given to their relevance in this horrific murder, but be assured more developments will evolve as things progress.

"One thing that's clear, St. Paul Homicide, acting on direct orders from Mayor Hanson, are coming to pick up two people suspected in the mass murder of fifteen people in St. Paul's Frog Town area. The two suspects' names and photos are Willie Roberts, he goes by the street name Toot; and then we have the one alleged to be the mastermind behind all this mess, Galen Davis, street name Dig a Hole. It's not known if either of these two are part of the three that were blown up on the porch, but DNA will reveal all that later. If not, please remember these two are considered extremely armed and dangerous! Do not, by any means, attempt to confront or detain them. If you see them, contact your local law agencies immediately."

After watching the same scenes for fifteen minutes, Dig a Hole got up, took the keys to the van and drove to a corner store. Stepping outside the van, he walked into the store and bought two pre-paid cell phones with a thousand minutes for each of them. Walking back out, he smashed his old cell and threw it in a sewer drain next to the van. Pulling back up to Pops house, he parked and proceeded to make three calls of importance.

CHAPTER 30

His first call was to his big sister Carla. Although he and she were raised separately, he always had a close bond with her.

"Hello, let me speak to Carla."

"Who's this?" asked the person on the other end.

"This Galen. Who is this?"

"Hey uncle Galen, this your niece Brittany!"

"Hey baby, how ya doing?"

"Okay. Are you here?"

"Naw. But I will be in a couple days, okay. Look, I need to holla at ya mom so put her on real fast okay."

"Okay. Love ya uncle Galen."

"Hello, Galen?"

"Yeah, baby."

"What's good bro."

"Not much. Look sis, I need ya and I need ya bad."

"Okay."

"Look sis I'm sending my wife Candyce down to ya. I need you to get her in a place ASAP, fully furnished and in an outsider's name with a car as well. I've got some problems and need to get low. She'll have more than enough money to hold ya'll down for the next ten years if need be, so you get it done now. I'll call and have her on the highway within the hour, okay."

Her response was nothing less than he expected from her. All she said was, "Anything for you baby bro. Be careful, I love you." "I love you too, and remember you haven't heard from me. Here's a number for me, only for emergencies. Go get a burn out and only call me from that, okay. Love ya." With that he hung up.

For a second Carla sat at her kitchen table with great concern for her baby brother. She knew he knew how to handle business but he was her heart and couldn't imagine anything happening to him. He had been there for her and her children when no one else was. He'd send money to her here and there, at times would even have someone show up out of the blue to give a care package only Galen could give. Not helping him in any way she could wasn't even an option.

She quickly got up and went to a store across town owned by Arabians to pick up two burn outs, one to start making things happen and one only for her brother. If they were being traced, she'd be damned if any fuck ups came on her behalf. She knew how to make her brother proud.

Making his next call, he informed Candyce of his plans and told her to take the half mil out the wall safe and to drive the Jaguar XK8 to his sister's and he would contact her then.

Adrenaline shot through Candyce's veins. She finally got the call she had been waiting for and jumped up off the couch and got herself together. She already had a suitcase packed and ready to go. She knew he wouldn't leave her behind and had it packed since their last conversation.

She did a cautionary scan around the house to make sure everything was secure and rushed out the front door. Before speeding off she took one last look at her beautiful home hoping it wouldn't be the last time she saw it.

His last call was to Gutter. After hearing that they were expecting Lord at any moment, Dig a Hole's mind went into overdrive, instructing them to rob him and take the mil ticket and work and met him in Kansas, not Des Moines. And not to use the phones because they were hot; to go get burn outs and call him when they were headed there.

After hanging up, Gutter informed Sinatra of the change in plans. Skeptical, but not one to question Dig a Hole's authority, they set forth to make it happen - waiting for the knock on the door.

When he completed all his calls, he walked back into Pops' house finding KeKe cooking chicken and spaghetti and Toot sitting with his eyes glued to the T.V., watching the same news broadcast over and over with a look of dismay in his eyes. Dig a Hole made a mental note to let his ass have it later.

Hearing Pops' car pull up, he immediately told Toot to change the channel, even though he was sure Pops saw the broadcast earlier. Walking in, whistling as he always did, Pops asked Dig a Hole to come out to the garage with him. Figuring this was unusual, he grabbed his 40 Glock on the way out.

Walking into the garage, he saw the greediest look yet in the eyes of Pops. Rubbing his palms together, Pops cleared his throat and said, "Look Young Blood. I ran a check on that ice and it's hotter than a hooker's pussy on Saturday night. I got the best I could for ya, and it's all I could. Basically a take-it-or-leave-it type of deal. Like I said, my people are a lil' leery right now. So $450,000 was all they'll come off of. Hell, it beats a blank."

Knowing Pops was full of shit and trying to take advantage of their current situation, not one to accept bullshit from any one, Dig a Hole looked Pops into his eyes and asked him, "Are you sure that's all you can get?" Basically giving him one last chance to reconsider the game he was playing.

Feeling the few drinks he had in him prior to returning home, Pops barked at him, "Did I stutter nigga?"

Not seeing the black gun until it was nearing his temple caused him to be slapped unconscious. Falling down knocking over his Craftsman's toolbox caused a loud noise which brought KeKe and Toot running out to them.

Witnessing the scene in front of them, and neither not sure what the fuck to say or do, Dig a Hole spoke first. "Toot go get some sheets and plastic bags out the house! KeKe, you have a choice to make, are you my bitch?"

"Daddy, you know I am."

"Well this piece of shit's trying to rob us and hinted if we didn't accept $100,000 for the jewelry he could get that for our reward on T.V." He thought he had to sugarcoat it so she could accept it. But little did he realize, none of it mattered, her loyalty was to him.

"Okay. What do you want me to do Daddy?"

"Shit, go see what the fuck's taking Toot so long."

Walking into the house and not seeing Toot in the kitchen made her go into the bedroom where the sheets were. She startled Toot as she walked into the room, seeing her caught him off guard. Realizing he was up to something, she asked what he just put in his back pocket. His hesitation only drew further suspicion, causing her to draw down on him. Pointing her seventeen shot Gauge Nine Millimeter at him she said "Empty your pockets or you're dead Toot."

Knowing damn well she meant every word, he threw his cell phone and wallet towards her, the only items in his pockets. Opening his wallet the first thing she saw was a picture of him and Courtney, the bitch she shot in the closet. Looking at him she threw his wallet back to him. She then picked up his cell phone, seeing him move she told him, "Slow your roll."

"Fuck that bitch. Who the fuck you think you are? Bitch, I'll rip your head off and piss down your throat." Toot said starting to charge at her.

It was at that moment the first shot went off, hitting him in his shoulder and knocking him to the ground. "Who's the bitch now, nigga? Huh? I can't hear ya. Sucka for love ass nigga. I enjoyed blowing Courtney's thick ass away. By the way, did she tell ya she was pregnant? Probably not, huh? Cuz it could have been any Joe Blow's," she said taunting him.

Dig a Hole rushed in, 40 Glock ready to pop. Seeing the scene he asked, "What happened?"

KeKe quickly filled him in and handed him the phone. Pressing redial, a 1-888 number came up. He could have sworn he recognized the number as he listened to the ringing in his ear. His suspicions were instantly confirmed when he heard the operator say, "Minneapolis Tip Line, may I help ya?"

Hanging up, he looked over at the person he once looked at as a brother but now considered him to be the worst piece of shit on earth. Walking over to Toot, he slapped him ruthlessly across his head with the butt of the Glock. He looked up at KeKe telling her to go start the fireplace and grab the duct tape out the garage; it was by where he tapped up Pops.

Dragging Toot's unconscious body into the living room, he taped his hands by securing them to his sides and taped his legs together as well. Dig a Hole brought him out of his sleep by pissing all over his face, telling him he was nothing more than a rat-faced, bitch ass nigga. And because of that, he was not only going to kill him, he was going after his mother, his three sisters and three other brothers he had, as well as his Pops. His whole family would pay for it. And as for his faggot ass son, his Junior, Lil' Toot, don't worry his brains would be fried just like his.

At that moment he lifted Toot, head first, into the raging fire that was in the fireplace. Smelling his flesh burning was a grotesque smell, causing KeKe to throw up instantaneously.

Holding his body by the waist so he couldn't wiggle out, Dig a Hole set the iron metal poker in the fire. Once Toot's body stopped wiggling, he pulled his pants down and took the red hot poker and crammed it up his faggot ass as far as it could possibly go, hoping to poke his heart out.

Putting the poker back in the fire, he walked out into the garage and stood quietly in the door watching KeKe as she stripped her father and was talking to him. As he sat taped to a workbench, hearing her cry he stepped back so to hear the real her.

"Remember you always told me I would be Daddy's little girl while shoving your long, black dick in my mouth? Remember that Daddy? Huh? Remember you told me I better not ever let no one have your pussy while you rammed your dirty hands in my six year old pussy? Huh, Dad?

"Or do you remember how for my ninth birthday you ripped my asshole wide open? Huh? Well, Pops guess what? I have a new Daddy and this is his pussy, his ass. And I thank you for teaching me how to suck dick, cuz I suck his so well. I've waited for so long for you to die so I wouldn't have to see your sick perverted eyes watch me every time I came around. But hey, today is your day! Want a blowjob Daddy?"

Laughing a sinister laugh she got on her knees and sucked her Pop's dick until it was rock hard. Seeing him enjoying the head, but still looking confused, she stood up. Looking at his enormous dick, the same one that had been traumatizing her since she was six years old, she reached out and grabbed the nail gun off the shelf. Recognizing what she held in her hand, he shook his head pleading with his eyes because his mouth was taped shut. Without hesitation she shot seven different nails into his long dick, leaving it nailed to the bench. Then looking in his tear-filled eyes, she raised the nail gun to shoot him in his eyes, but not before Dig a Hole said, "Hold on baby."

Coming out of her daze she turned toward his voice. Seeing him hand her the red hot poker, she smiled knowing he understood. Looking at her, he said, "Handle yours baby!" Turning around she pierced the poker through each of his eyeballs, allowing the hot poker to go all the way through his entire head.

Realizing she had tears streaming down her face, she turned and headed back into the house feeling relieved, leaving both the poker and her memories in the garage.

Walking back into the house and seeing Toot's body half way in the fireplace, she looked at Dig a Hole and said, "What now Daddy?"

To which he replied, "Let's shake this bitch down. I know he's got some cash here." Walking off looking first in the bedroom, he immediately found a hidden room inside the closet because her bitch ass father didn't close the hidden door all the way.

Going inside the tiny but neat place, he saw a huge blue and gray bag in the corner. After opening it up, he saw exactly what he hoped it would be - cash money. Inside the bag were bundles upon bundles of money. Placing the bag on a stand in the middle of the room, he continued to look around, finding a suitcase. Inside the suitcase was numerous diamonds of various shapes and sizes. Closing the case and grabbing the duffel bag, he made his way out the closet and started heading toward the door while calling KeKe from out the basement. Coming up the stairs he gave her a look they both understood meant, "Let's go!"

CHAPTER *31*

Sitting in the hotel waiting on Lord to come make the purchase, Sinatra and Gutter talked in hushed tones trying to figure out if Lord would come alone or if he'd bring security. Either way they'd find a way to get the upper hand, knowing the element of surprise was in their favor. Getting up to go into the restroom, Gutter heard the knock on the door before Sinatra did. Giving Sinatra the heads-up, he cocked his 9mm and walked to the door. Looking out the peep hole he asked, "Who is it?"

"It's Lord, brother!"

Taking the chain off and unlocking the locks, Gutter opened the door to a smiling ass yellow bitch standing next to Lord.

Sinatra asked, "Ya'll going to come in or stand in the hall all day!"

Laughing the bitch says, "You got to move out the way. You expect me to squeeze all this ass past you?"

Stepping in the room, Gutter noticed neither of them was carrying a bag which should have held the money. Securing the door behind them, he walked up behind Lord and knocked him out cold with the butt of his pistol, while Sinatra drew down instantly on the yellow bitch.

Realizing what was going down, she spoke first saying, "I aint got shit to do with this. He just asked me to ride with him."

Not wasting a second Gutter told her to lie on the ground, face down, while he finished tying Lord up. Hearing her cry only enraged Gutter so he told her, "Shut the fuck up before I give ya a reason to cry." Noticing she had a fat ass, he knew he'd taste her yellow ass before he killed her.

After making sure both Lord and the bitch were secured, Sinatra proceeded to interrogate her, but not before he took the blunt Gutter was smoking and put it out inside her ear letting her know he didn't give a fuck about her fears or tears and that this wasn't a game. After fifteen minutes of squirming she settled down and just looked terrified as Gutter stood over her. Talking to Sinatra, she wasn't able to make out exactly what it was he was saying due to the ear trauma she just received. But what she did know, by the way he constantly held his dick and kept looking at her, is that he wanted to fuck her. Thinking this could be her way out of the situation alive she decided to go with the flow.

Hearing Lord moving around inside the bathtub drew both Sinatra and Gutter's attention away from their devious sexual thoughts. Walking into the bathroom they found an alert Lord staring at the ceiling. Sinatra took the tape out his mouth and before he could say a word Lord blurted out, "Do you niggas realize who the fuck I am? Ya'll done signed your death warrant!"

Not one for all the chitchat, Gutter stepped up and slapped him with the pistol, knocking his head back into the side of the tub. "Let's get this hoe ass nigga out the tub and give him a lil' understanding. See if he can talk shit with his head in the shitter."

Smiling as he caught on to what Gutter meant, Sinatra grabbed Lord by the legs and Gutter grabbed him by the arms hoisting his limp body onto the floor. Grabbing him by the throat, Gutter pushed his unconscious head into the toilet. The cold water revived him enough to comprehend that his efforts to fight back were useless. Just when he felt like passing out, he was brought up for air, but just enough to get two good breaths, then he was submerged again.

After about four times Sinatra said, "Enough," and gave Gutter the signal that it was time to get back to bizness. Upon bringing his head out the toilet, they noticed he was no longer resisting. His eyes remained open and he looked dead.

Panicking because he got carried away and may have killed the nigga before getting what they came for, Sinatra asked, "Now what we going to do?"

"We're going to go make that bitch tell us where it's at."

CHAPTER 32

Taking off in the van, Dig a Hole asked KeKe where they could get a rental car. "I think there's an Enterprise up there on Johnson Parkway," she said.

"Look baby. I want you to go get us another conversion van. Get it in your name because you have a valid license with that name. I'm going to drop you off at the rental agency and then I'm going to go take the plates off this van and leave it parked here at the grocery store, okay. You come back here to scoop me up."

"Gotcha, Daddy."

"KeKe, are you okay? I mean, I saw the little demonstration

you put on back there wit your Pops."

"Daddy, I've never felt more relieved in my life because one can't know of skeletons in my closet if there are no longer any skeletons to be found."

"Alright then, let's get the fuck away from this bad luck ass town."

CHAPTER 33

"Sergeant Jackson, can we please get a statement from you about the events that have taken place over the last week involving the fifteen bodies discovered in St. Paul; and are there any ties to the eighteen people killed in a raid in north Minneapolis? Please, the public has a right to know." A reporter from Kare 11 asked as she shoved a microphone in his face.

"Okay. Okay," Jackson repeated. "I'll give you as much as I can. But you need to understand there is an intensive investigation going on and right now too much media coverage could hinder the apprehension of our prime suspects. But, what I will tell you is there's a rogue group of men running rampant through our city who have no sort of respect for human life. They are being led by an individual who has an extensive criminal history and should have been locked up with the key thrown away years ago.

I will not rest until I know one of two things. One, that Galen Davis is either identified as one of the victims of the raid on 26th and Colfax, or that he's in jail. Our Coroner is processing the bodies as fast as he can. The Mayor, along with the Governor, has given us unlimited resources to do whatever is necessary to catch these killers. That's all for now."

Walking away to his squad car feeling helpless and indifferent, with very few leads, and an opportunity for the career advancement of a lifetime quickly fading, he knew time was a luxury he didn't have: the "Powers That Be" wanted results.

CHAPTER 34

Upon hearing the news of the deaths of Mr. Gray and Mr. Brown, The Coalition found themselves once again having to convene. Speaking first, Mr. Red asked, "Do we have any ideal what the hell went down? Also, do we know if the Minneapolis P.D. is on to our operation? They've identified Mr. Gray and Mr. Brown. What info do we have as of right now?"

Mr. Orange, the most informed member, primarily because he rose rank quickly to Sergeant due to a lack of minority officers within Ohio, reported, "Well, what we do know is the phone number of Corleone's last call was to a Keyawna Jackson. She's an African American female, one-hundred-forty-five pounds, five-feet-eight-inches tall, caramel complected, no criminal record but an extensive history with our subject of interest, Galen Davis.

Her last known address is the place we had staked out. It mysteriously caught fire the same day Gray and Brown were killed. As of yet, Minneapolis P.D. hasn't implicated her in any of the crimes, nor does she appear to be a person of interest. At least not right now, so that's to our advantage. Furthermore, she has a twin sister who is a preacher. It's my personal belief wherever we find her, we'll find Dig a Hole."

He continued saying, "She has a father in Denver and her mother is deceased. The father is an ex-Black Panther with a shady background. I believe Corleone and Steele to be dead, as well. My guess is that Keyawna and Dig a Hole are laying lower than low right.

"It's to our advantage that we know about his ties to Keyawna, but with the attention this is drawing, it won't take investigators long before they go look into Dig a Hole's prison records and see she was on his visiting list. So does anyone have any suggestions?"

"I suggest we stake out her father's house and do a national check on car rental agencies. Who knows? They might make a mistake under the impression she hasn't been added to the equation. Check all hotel listings and go speak with her sister as well. We have to catch them before the other forces do, and make sure they meet an excruciatingly painful demise. Best believe they're traveling with a load of cash," exclaimed Mr. Yellow.

Now seeing his opportunity to express his thoughts, Mr. Blue threw a plan on the table. "Look. We all feel terrible about Gray and Brown, but the reality is we all know there are risks to this life we've chosen. And behind every action, there's a reaction. Sometimes the consequences and repercussions behind our actions aren't ones we like, but that doesn't mean go run off and make situations worse. It means just the opposite. We need to be more methodical with everything we do from here on out. We should never have let them go up there without first knowing what they were up against.

"Hell, from the reports I've both seen and heard, them ganstas they were onto were a small militia. They didn't stand a chance! So, all I'm saying is this - if we all don't go into this with level heads, then I'm walking away. There's nothing we can do to bring our boys back, so we look forward to what we can do. And that's making sure their families are taken care of. So rather than going out seeking revenge like some vigilantes, let's go complete the mission that got us into this whole mess, retrieving our money and dope. Now, is there anyone who has any other thoughts besides those I just laid out?

GET DOWN OR LAY DOWN

"With no one speaking up, I'll assume we're all in agreement. So here's the next move. Red and Black, you two will take the father's place. Green and Yellow, ya'll go back to Minneapolis, question the sister, put your ear to the street and see if we can bring forth some useful info. Orange, you do all the checks with the rental cars and hotels, and I'll look into how much the Minneapolis P.D. knows about our guys and reach out to their wives, reminding them to keep their mouths shut and say they have no idea why their husbands were up north. We all stay in touch daily with Orange, especially all developments, minor or major. Okay?"

CHAPTER 35

Walking into the office of the Violent Crimes and Homicide Unit in Minneapolis, Sergeant Jackson was greeted by three FBI agents and two ATF agents.

"Hello. We're agents from the FBI. I'm Senior Agent Tom Peters, these two are Special Agents Thomas and Mento. Along with us are Agent Wilson and Agent Jabowski from the ATF. We've been assigned to takeover the St. Paul and Minneapolis homicides on a joint venture. This seems to be a lil' out of the State's league so if ya'll relinquish any and all evidence and files you have of relevance to these cases ASAP, we'll be on our way." Holding papers up for Sergeant Jackson to see he continued, "Here are the orders from the Governor and U.S. Attorney General themselves. I'm sure you gentlemen will assist us in getting all the stated items in a timely manner."

Saying no more, they left business cards and walked out, leaving Jackson stuck like a crackhead after his first big blast.

CHAPTER 36

Both with their game faces on, Sinatra and Gutter came back into the room and sat the redbone up on the bed, taking the tape off her mouth they asked her what her name is.

"Dominique," was all she said.

"Look Dominique, your friend is dead, and if you want to leave this room alive you'll cooperate with us. Do you understand what I'm saying to you?" Looking into her eyes to emphasize his seriousness, Gutter held his stare. If the eyes were the windows to the soul, then this bitch in front of him didn't have one.

Nodding her head in compliance, but thinking to herself she

really didn't care if she did die because they took her reason for living. Lord was her heart and soul. Not just that, her husband. At this point, she would do whatever necessary to live another day to see to it these dudes paid for the shit they pulled on her husband.

Sinatra walked over to her and asked, "What was the plans wit the money? And before you reply, let me tell you I will do whatever is needed to extract this info from you, so don't play no game bitch."

"Okay. All I know is we was suppose to meet some dudes here, check out some stuff and if everything was cool we were suppose to meet Cantrell at the mini-mart on 69th."

"Who's Cantrell?" asked Sinatra.

"He's his brother. He has the money there."

Slapping her, Sinatra spit in her face saying, "Bitch if you lying, you're one dead motherfucker." Just then the phone rang.

Answering it Gutter said, "What it do?"

"What's really good homeboy?" KeKe asked.

"Not a thang." Sinatra calmly replied.

"Well, Dig asks is everything, everything or what?"

"You tell him we're on our way out the door to handle that now."

"Check this out. Instead of Des Moines, let's meet in Kansas

City. Check into the Best Western on Spokane and don't make any calls back up to Minnesota. It's hot, ya feel me? So, we'll see ya'll by 8:00 pm right?"

"Yea, we'll be there." He assured her.

"Drive careful." She said before hanging up.

"Bogus or nothing." Looking at Dominique, Gutter said to Sinatra, "Before we go I got to fuck this bitch. I know you want some, don't ya?"

"I'm good. I just want to hit this lick and get out of here. So hurry up." Sinatra said shaking his head.

With no more to be said Gutter barked at Dominique saying, "Bitch you about to get the best fucken you ever had." Taking no time to cut the tape off her hands, he stripped her asshole naked, telling her to bend over for an ass shot. Afraid of what he'd do if she resisted she willingly complied, just waiting on him to slip.

Looking at her fat ass from behind, he roughly forced his two fingers inside her asshole. Hearing her gasp only enticed him more. Pulling his fingers out, he quickly discarded his clothes and rammed his rock-hard dick inside her asshole. He fucked her rough and hard as he smacked her brutally on her ass and savagely pulled her hair, the whole time telling her she better not let out a peep of noise.

Disgusted by the brutality of it all, Sinatra went into the

bathroom to put Lord into the tub and take a shit.

Feeling himself about to nut, Gutter pulled out and ordered Dominique to turn around and suck him off. She obligingly did as instructed, sucking his cock the way she would suck her husband's and sent him into a daze making him forget where he was at and what he was really suppose to be doing.

Instead of watching her, he stood up with his head laid back, eyes toward the roof, moaning about how good the head was. Seeing the opportunity to make a play for the gun that lay inches from her reach, she knew this opportunity may never present itself again and started licking her way down to his balls knowing this would really relax him even more.

As she began to tickle in between his balls with her tongue, she grabbed his Colt Commander 45. In a swift and hard upward motion she thrust the hard, cold steel onto his nut sack causing him to fall to the floor swearing. Sinatra ran out the bathroom only to be staring down the barrel of a 45 and looking into the eyes of a scorned woman.

CHAPTER 37

Pulling up in the parking lot of a Motel 6 in Kansas City, KeKe parked the rented 2009 Ford Conversion Van away from the open spots near the front entrance. Before getting out she took a moment to look into the review mirror to make sure her Mac lip gloss was intact, just in case a sucker was working the front desk. She didn't need to but she got off by putting on a show and didn't want to miss an opportunity should one present itself.

Satisfied with what she saw she winked at Dig a Hole and glided out of the van with the confidence as if she was walking on a catwalk. KeKe sashayed her way inside the motel knowing he was devouring every single step that she took. She may not be his woman anymore but she knew she had the number-one-bitch-in-the-hood spot on lock and was certain he was rubbing his dick right now just by watching her perform for him. She got wet just thinking about the power of her pussy.

Once inside she immediately locked eyes with the stunning female behind the counter. She was absolutely gorgeous, just how she liked it. She had beautiful full lips, plump, round tits and long blond hair. Given different circumstances she would have been thrown off guard by this amazing beauty had she not been so well-trained by Dig a Hole.

As she approached the counter she immediately felt the chick's vibe and knew this was going to be a piece of cake: she wouldn't even need to take out one of her alias ids to rent a single room. Although not many words were spoken during the transaction it was obvious there was an intense sexual attraction as the clerk conveniently told KeKe's alias Keyshia that should she need anything, anything at all, she would be working until 8:00 that night.

As the clerk turned around to rip the room receipt off the printer she made sure she poked her donk out for KeKe to take it all in. After she turned around KeKe replied, "Oh you can bet on that baby girl," and made sure she slowly glided her perfectly manicured hand over hers as she took the receipt from her.

Walking away she couldn't help but laugh to herself, if there was any time she would definitely pay Ms. Pretty a visit knowing damn well she would not only get some head, she would take that bitch for all she had. Hell to her a trick was a trick, it didn't matter if they had a dick or not. Actually bitches were easier to knock off then most dudes, they gave up far easier and way faster.

But it was whatever with her. Regardless, she would get her rocks off in more ways than one. She knew by the way she heard Dig a Hole talking to Candyce that it was a wrap emotionally between them. It would only be a matter of time before he left her alone all together. She had to prepare herself and come up by any means necessary. That's the kind of bitch she's been bred to be – Bogus for life.

Coming back out she slinked back into the van the way she had left and handed the room keys to Dig a Hole. Thinking it would be better for him not to go in any public places if it could be avoided, he sent her in to put the suitcases of money and jewelry up.

Coming right back out, they headed across town to check into the Best Western across from the Super 8. It was only 4:30 pm and they still had hours before they were to meet up with Sinatra and Gutter.

CHAPTER 38

Looking at Dominique to see if he could see any weaknesses but not seeing any, he thought it would be best to try to talk her down knowing she wouldn't listen to a thang Gutter had to say after violating her the way he did. Looking down at Gutter, Sinatra's only thoughts besides killing this hoe was killing that trick ass nigga because things were only getting worse due to his foolishness.

With flashes of memories of her husband racing through her mind -a rage unlike any other she had felt in her entire life - Dominique picked up a pillow and placed the gun in front of it, firing it straight into Gutter's head. The pillow did its job because the gun shot was barely heard.

Upon seeing his lifeless body drop, she aimed the gun at Sinatra. Seeing the fear in his eyes, she couldn't help but think to herself how helpless he looked with his hands raised like he was in school. How could such a coward get away with killing her world so easily?

Becoming even more furious at this notion, she blanked out into a psychotic blur and calmly and gently ordered, "Get on your hands and knees bitch ass nigga."

Stuttering, trying to muster up all the courage he could, he looked directly in her burning eyes and said, "Fuck you bitch," while attempting to get up. He saw the switch go off inside her and didn't waiver, knew he wouldn't bow down to no bitch regardless of the circumstances.

She pointed the gun at his groin area laughing and said, "So you're Mr. Tough Guy, huh? You got balls? I'll give it to ya," and fired a single shot. Hitting him in his nut sack, she watched him tumble over and said, "You don't have none anymore." She walked over, placed the pillow over his head and squeezed the remaining bullets into his dome before he got the chance to move.

Wasting no time, instinct kicked in, and she feverishly searched the room, finding two hundred and eighty kilos in the closet closest to the door. She quickly put a few of the bricks in her Coach purse, silently thanking herself for choosing a bigger bag than normal tonight.

After packing both her purse and a suitcase she found, she moved quickly into the bathroom to kiss her husband their final goodbye. For a brief moment she almost put the gun to her own head but suddenly realized that although she had temporarily avenged her husband's death, she knew these two were just guppies, there were bigger fish to fry. Hell hath no fury like a woman scorned.

Every step she took away from her husband's dead body was one step closer to her in losing her mind. She wanted to lie on his body until she had to be pried off by the paramedics, but instead pulled strength from within and walked away without looking back.

CHAPTER 39

Within the safe comforts of the Best Western, Dig a Hole replayed the events that had taken place over the last seventy-two hours. Never one to panic or make irrational decisions, he meticulously plotted his next moves. Realizing he was on the hot sheet of every law enforcement agency across the U.S., and probably abroad as well, he knew being inconspicuous was a must. Never sleeping in the same place twice and switching cars after every layover was mandatory, as well as never letting anyone know his next move, even if they were with him.

Feeling his stomach growl, he realized it had been over a day since he'd eaten a decent meal. Recognizing this and knowing this would give him ample time to make some of the important calls he needed to make, he instructed to KeKe, "Why don't you go grab us some chicken and some of that fire ass dirty rice they got out at Popeye's. Don't forget the mash potatoes and corn."

"Dang baby, I already know. You aint got to tell me how to feed you." Knowing he didn't like to hear himself tell a bitch anything twice she rushed up off her chair. Getting up to leave she walked over to give him a kiss, but not before grabbing her pistol and placing it inside her Fendi purse.

Not feeling like resting, Dig a Hole recalled a car he'd seen for sale down the street from the hotel. Stopping her before she could get out the door he said, "Hold up baby. I'm going to have you drop me off down the street so I can check out this other whip. That way we can return the rental here in Kansas."

"Okay, sounds good baby."

Grabbing his 40 Cal, the two of them left out to go take care of their bizness.

CHAPTER 40

Back in Minneapolis, Homicide Detective Jackson received a call from Chicago's Homicide Squad inquiring about the open cases of the recent murders of the officers and civilians. It pissed him off that the Feds stepped in and halted his opportunity to receive his promotion, so he returned the call more out of curiosity. "Hello, may I speak with Lieutenant Malone?"

"This is Malone speaking. Who may I ask is calling?"

"This is Sergeant Jackson, Minneapolis Homicide. I received a message from you inquiring about the multiple homicide that's taken place over the last seventy-two hours!"

"Yeah, it seems to have run down our way. We found three

bodies in a hotel room; two of which belonged to the gang ya'll have interest in and the other has ties to Minnesota but is a big narcotics dealer down here. We received a call from the hotel saying gunshots were heard from the room next to where these murders happened. Upon entering the room we found one male naked from the waist down and the other with what appeared to be a gunshot wound to the head.

"The half-naked one had multiple gunshot wounds to the head. The killer attempted to hide the noise by muffling the gun with a pillow that was found at the scene, as well as several other firearms. The third body was found in the bathtub. We're not sure of the cause of death. It appears to be strangulation; we won't be sure until an autopsy is completed.

"We ran ballistics and fingerprint analysis, and the prints match the two victims who died by the gunshot wounds that night. Upon further investigation, we found their car in the parking lot with Minnesota tabs, 052 GYN; a 2007 Acura Legend registered to a Valerie Jacobs."

While hearing all this, Jackson patiently took notes and waited to get the main question in that was on his mind. "Did you find anyone by the name of Galen Davis?"

"As of yet, no. But we're running a thorough check of all the guests that are checked into the hotel. So we'll keep you updated on any new developments on this case. I'm sure there is room for another brother to get a piece of the spotlight as well. Right, brother?"

After hanging up the phone, Jackson contemplated whether he should forward the info onto the Feds and let them steal his opportunity for advancement or continue to try to solve these murders on his own? Deciding he wasn't going to let the prospect pass him by, he placed Lieutenant Malone's message in the shredder and his notes in his suitcase.

CHAPTER 41

After running KeKe's name in the nationwide search for rental cars, Mr. Blue received a hit almost immediately. He placed a call to Mr. Red and Mr. Black to notify them of his findings.

"Right here baby! Damn, you done passed the motherfucker. Can't you hear? I said, right here and your stupid ass keep rolling," screamed Dig a Hole.

"Dang, Boo I can go back!" Backing up a half a block instead of turning around, KeKe pulled into the lot. Pissed about being checked by him and mad at herself for making him angry, she let Dig a Hole out and peeled out aggressively back into the traffic, not seeing the Traffic Cop across the street at the Coffee Shop.

Seeing the van violate multiple traffic laws and noticing it had Colorado plates, Officer Grisby decided he'd roll down on her and give her a couple citations; normally he'd let it slide, but he hadn't made his quota for the month. Hitting his emergency response lights, he initiated the stop.

Seeing the squad car jump behind her, KeKe pulled over - happy and mad at the same time. Happy Dig a Hole wasn't in the car, and mad because out of anger she made a stupid mistake that, had he been in the van, could have cost them everything.

From down the block Dig a Hole watched as the squad car raced out behind the van, pulling it over. He watched for several minutes, and not seeing any other squads come confirmed his suspicion she'd gotten pulled for some traffic shit. Walking into the dealer's office he told him he wanted to purchase the 2005 Mercury Sable; it was both plain and inconspicuous enough to not be noticed. Without even test driving it, he paid for the car and left.

Going to the Motel 6 to retrieve his stash, he'd been having mixed feelings and wanted to have a vehicle with his stash ready to go upon demand. Seeing that the money and jewelry was as

he'd left it, he left to go to an auto shop to request a complete
tune-up and new tires. While waiting for his car to be serviced,
he decided to place his much-needed calls, first to Candyce, then
to his Cuban homie in Miami.

CHAPTER 42

To Mr. Orange's surprise his inquiries into locating KeKe paid off almost instantly. It came through on the wire that she was pulled over in Kansas City in a rented conversion van. The plates of the van came back to a rental agency in Denver. Without delay, he redirected Mr. Red and Mr. Black to Kansas, advising them to search all the hotels in the area for the van. His next call was to Mr. Green and Mr. Yellow, instructing them to question Keyawsha, KeKe's twin, about relatives in other states.

"Now look, Mr. Red, we want to locate and apprehend the suspects in hopes that they're traveling wit the money. She was alone during the traffic stop, so hopefully she's confident that we're not on to her and she'll let her guard down. I want ya'll to be as inconspicuous as possible and use extreme caution when you encounter them. Keep in mind that over the last week they've been involved in at least twenty homicides, so they have nothing to lose. Take no chances."

"I copy that, Mr. Orange, and will follow your advice to the letter. I'm hoping to catch her alone and either force her to provide us with the info on how to obtain the package, or take us to it. We'll call and check in as soon as we hit the city."

CHAPTER 43

Digging his phone out his pocket so he could call Candyce, Dig a Hole received a call from KeKe.

"Hello?"

"What's good, baby girl?"

"Shit, just waiting on this dirty rice to get done. Check this out. After I dropped you off I got pulled over by a rookie cop. He wasn't on shit, just wanted his quota."

Smiling, Dig a Hole was wondering if she would tell him about the traffic stop. Because, had she not, he'd have been skeptical of her intentions and she would have been subject to an untimely termination.

"Okay, dig this. Since they done stopped the van, it's time to switch up anyway. Take it to the rental car place and swap it in for a Navigator, okay?"

"Alright, I'm on it. Where you at?"

"I'm at the room baby."

"Did you like the car? Well, I guess not if you're having me get another one. Sorry for asking stupid questions Daddy."

"Enough said. Handle that and see ya when ya get back. The guys will be here shortly."

"Okay," was all she said. Hanging up she cussed herself out for once again acting out of place. Now was not the time to start fucking up and risking the chance of having Dig a Hole second guess her. At any moment all he had to do was think she was weak and he'd take her out.

Irritated and eager to get back to him she flipped on the cashier and said, "Hurry the fuck up you retarded ass bitch, my man is hungry!"

Finally able to make his calls, he dialed Candyce. She answered on the first ring. "Hello!"

"Hey gorgeous, how are you?"

"I'm stressing baby and really need to see you. Where you

at?"

"Look, I'm in the Florida Keys. I want you to catch a plane to Miami, take a boat over to the Keys and we'll meet at the Fair Born Hotel, okay? Call me as soon as you're heading to the Keys, alright?"

"Okay. Should I bring anything?"

"Just a lil' money. Leave the rest with Carla to put up. Did she get you that place?"

"Yeah, it's straight, but it don't matter right now: I'm on my way to see you and that's all that matters to me right now."

"That's right gorgeous, just relax and be on the next thang smoking heading this way."

"Alright, I'll see you then. Galen, I love you!"

"I know you do. I love you too Candyce."

After handing up the phone, Dig a Hole noticed two familiar faces on the raggedy T.V. screen in the corner of the waiting room, Gutter and Sinatra. Turning up the volume, he learned their bodies were discovered in the hotel room, and another body as well, Lord's. Confused, he was not sure how that happened, but he was positive it was time to hit the road ASAP.

He called Cuban Joe, an old acquaintance from Stillwater Prison. Cuban Joe had been in prison with Dig a Hole and was his connect inside the joint with every thang from fuck books to shanks, you name it Cuban Joe had a resource to obtain it.

Many days they walked the prison yard, Dig a Hole listening as Joe told him of the ways of his country. About how Castro hated America and how revolutionaries such as the Black Panthers and the Black Liberation Army sought refuge from America over there. No matter your crime, they wouldn't extradite, especially if you had money to offer. Dig a Hole thought there was no better time than now than to utilize Joe's resources.

"Joe my friend, long time no hear from."

"Hey Dig a Hole. So what do I owe the pleasure of this call? I see you are a very important person now a days. I've seen you and your people on every channel in the country. I hope you're laid back like a perm, because if them people get their greasy palms on you you'll be stretched out like a research monkey! Ha, ha."

"Well, my nigga, you're right. I'm hotter than the sun right now, but you're wrong about the stretching me out part. I have every intention of being my own Judge and Jury. So when these bitch made mutherfuckers roll down on me, they better come ready to get down or lay down. Because laying it down just aint an option for me. But you don't hear me though."

"Oh Amigo, I hear and feel ya. What can I do for you?"

"Remember the talks we had about Cuba?"

"Yeah of course I do."

"Well, can you make some arrangements to get me safe

passageway there, ASAP?"

"Look, everything is negotiable."

"Okay. Make it happen. I'll contact you at 3:00 pm tomorrow. Will we be ready to roll?"

"Not only will your ride be ready, I'll have you a place to stay there and everything set up. You'll just have to grease the General's hand and that will be sufficient enough to allow you entry, okay?"

"Sounds good my homie. I got a lil' something special just for you. See you then." Hanging up the phone, he walked into the bay area to check on his car. Seeing it was completed, he tipped the mechanic and made his way to the gas station before heading back to the hotel.

CHAPTER 44

Leaving Popeye's, KeKe pulled into Enterprise rental car, hoping it would be a young male working so she could work her magic. To her misfortune, it was an old gray-haired white man. Walking in she politely informed him of her situation, telling him she was traveling from Denver and the van was needed for room because they had kids at the time. The space is no longer needed so she'd like to get a Lincoln Navigator.

"That will be no problem, Miss. I'll need your driver's license and credit card." Handing him her license, he walked to the other end of the counter and proceeded to do the paperwork. After entering her name into the computer, it immediately was red flagged: meaning contact law enforcement. Not wanting to draw suspicion he walked back to KeKe and informed her he just had two Navigators brought back in, and she was more than welcome to wait for them to be thoroughly cleaned out and washed.

Being impatient, KeKe asked could she reserve one and come back in an hour or two. Noticing her reluctance to stay, he made one last effort to keep contact, "Okay. I assume being a visitor, you're staying at a hotel, correct?"

"Yeah, I'm staying at the Best Western, room --," catching herself, she corrected herself by saying, "I'll just call back in an hour. Give me a bizness card."

Giving her time to leave the lot, Clifford, the car rental assistant, anxiously called the number that was on the computer to report KeKe's whereabouts in hopes of adding some excitement to his life.

CHAPTER 45

After filling up, Dig a Hole decided it was best to just leave out ahead of KeKe, stalling her for a couple hours, giving himself a few hours distance hoping she didn't see the news of Gutter and Sinatra. Dig a Hole's survival always came from following his first mind, it never led him wrong. And his mind had been telling him to put some more distance between him and the Midwest. Putting the car on cruise control, seatbelt on, he headed south.

CHAPTER 46

Mr. Orange was ecstatic when he received the call from an overanxious salesclerk from Enterprise rental car in Kansas. They were so close to recovering their money and merchandise and putting this whole incident behind them: after notifying Mr. Black and Mr. Red as to where KeKe was staying, he sat patiently waiting on the call saying it's over.

CHAPTER 47

Driving back to the hotel, KeKe stopped to purchase some blunts and some condoms. Her pussy was hot and she wasn't going to settle for Dig a Hole's lame ass excuse, "Aint no hubcaps," because when he wanted to fuck, he did, with or without condoms. Only this time she was gonna poke holes in every last one of them.

Getting back into the van she turned on her favorite CD, Young Jeezy and Keyshia Cole's "I Must Be Dreaming," and headed across the street to the room. Doing as Dig a Hole always taught her, she circled the parking lot looking for anything abnormal. It wasn't until her second time around she saw two brothers sitting in an unmarked car looking suspicious. Not taking any chances, she pulled back out the lot. Looking into the rearview she noticed they pulled off and were directly behind her.

Keeping her cool, she turned her blinker on signaling a left turn. The other car attempted to pull in front, blocking her turning lane. Steering out of their way, she floored the van straight ahead with them in full pursuit. Picking up her phone, pressing Dig a Hole's number on speed dial, she prayed he had it on.

Answering on the third or fourth ring, he said, "What up."

"Baby! Baby, they're on us! You got to get out of there. Now!"

"Calm down. Who's on us? The Law?"

"Yes, they're all over the hotel. I'm on a high-speed chase right now. They were sitting in the parking lot."

"Okay, KeKe. Where are you now?"

"I'm heading toward the Express Way, on Van Buren."

"Do you think you can shake them?"

"I don't know. So far I can only see one car."

"So what is it, a squad car?"

"No, an unmarked."

"Well how do you know it's the fucken police? Pull into a parking lot of a mall, grocery store, whatever. You got your pistol with you, right?"

"Yes."

"Well pull in, get out, and if it's the Law you don't have any warrants you were just pulled over. And if it's Jack Boys' who marked us because of our out-of-state plates, then deal with it accordingly. You hear me?"

"Yea Daddy, I gotcha." Just the smooth sound of his confident voice was reassuring enough to calm herself and get back focused again. What he didn't realize, nor understand, was that her fear wasn't for her, it was for him. Seeing a supermarket up ahead, she slowed down just enough to swoop into the parking lot without signaling, causing her tail to bypass their turn. Appearing she lost them, she floored the van into a parking space and proceeded to exit the vehicle.

Heading toward the entrance of the store, she was almost run over by the black unmarked car; it came speeding out of nowhere. Not hesitating, she grabbed her nine millimeter sig saur out her purse and let that bitch bark. Her first shot went through the windshield, hitting the driver in the head causing the vehicle to swerve into a line of grocery carts.

As she continued to fire, she didn't notice the passenger had rolled out of his vehicle, and by the time she did, it was too late. Turning around she saw him as he squeezed two quick shots off, hitting her high in the chest. Feeling the hot lead hit her was all she felt, she was dead before she hit the ground. Running over to her lifeless corpse, Mr. Black emptied three more shots into her face. Grabbing her purse, he headed toward the van she had just gotten out of, and pulled out the lot fast, trying to distance himself from the scene. He fumed over the loss of his partner, making a vow to kill Dig a Hole for this.

The sound of a phone ringing brought him out of his daze. Digging into her purse to retrieve her phone he saw Dig a Hole's name on the caller I.D. "Hello, Mr. Notorious Dig a Hole!"

"Oh yeah? Who the fuck is this, fuck boy?" Dig a Hole replied.

"Well. This is your worst nightmare. You're way out your league homeboy. You just added capital murder to your resume. But don't worry, by nightfall none of it will matter because you'll be in a fucken hole."

"So that's how ya feel? Well I'll tell you what. Bring the fucken Marine Corps because you State bitches aint ready. I'll continue to send you hoes to ya maker." Those were the last words Dig a Hole said before hanging up.

He took the battery out of his phone and threw it out the window; laughing to himself as he thought about KeKe, thinking, "Better her than me." He believed in the Game God's prophesy because nature rewarded the strong and killed off the weak. Seeing he was the last one riding, he knew the saying to be true.

Calling Mr. Orange from his own phone, Mr. Black relayed the current situation and the fact that he had spoke to Dig a Hole himself. Knowing he wasn't sitting around because he had checked KeKe's call log and discovered that she had spoken with him during their chase, Mr. Orange thought enough was enough. They'd lost three officers from their coalition's eight, and he felt it was best to regroup and restrategize the whole scenario.

"Come on home, Mr. Black. All we're going to end up doing is getting further entangled in his web of destruction. We'll find a way to get back, we always do."

"Yea, alright," was Mr. Black's reply, hanging up the phone just as he entered a liquor store.

CHAPTER 48

Back in Minnesota, the Feds, along with the help of the ATF had turned the heat up in the city. Shaking any and every body down, investigating every lead, they left no stone unturned. With a half-million-dollar bounty on Dig a Hole alone, the Tip Line stayed ringing.

The Tip Line is what led to Candyce. Surveillance had been placed on her and she almost pulled off the whole charade until she made an error, at least in the Feds' eye: she left town. Not knowing better – meaning Galen not considering these extremes with his true family - she trapped herself into being tailed, and brought them to Dig a Hole's sister. Special Agents Wilson and

Jabowski sat patiently as they watched from down the block, seeing Candyce embrace several people they believed to be Dig a Hole's family. This led them to think she was heading away for a while. Just as they figured this, she jumped on the highway heading south.

Trailing her at a distance, trying to remain out of sight, they had no idea that Candyce was no fool. Galen may have not trained her as he did to all his bust downs in the streets, he didn't have to as Candyce fed off her natural instincts as his Queen, and as a woman in love and with child. Although she had innocent ways, she was still very perceptive to what her man would have wanted her to do and instinctively saw them shadowing her as she jumped on the Express Way. Seeing that they were indeed still following her, she contemplated her next move. But as another hour and a half passed and they were still on her trail, she called Dig a Hole, praying they didn't have her phone tapped.

Answering on the second ring, sounding imperturbable as always saying, "Hey lil' Momma! So how's things going?"

"Not good Daddy. I left Carla's a couple hours ago and it seems that I've picked up a tail. They've been with me since Peoria. I'm scared baby, what should I do? I thought I could prove to you that I could shake them on my own, but I can't do it without your guidance. I am so sorry. I just wanted to get to you as fast I could, I should have been thinking more clearly."

Thinking fast, Dig a Hole revised the plan. "Look baby, I want more than anything for you and our babies to be here with me, but here's what you need to do. Being that they won't shake loose, stop at the next rest stop, okay? Call me from there. I'll give you instructions from there, okay?"

"Okay Daddy. I'm so sorry, I should of been called."

"It's okay. Just do as I asked you. Bye." With that he hung up and dialed the Cuban homeboy in Miami to make sure everything was both clear and set up.

"What's up my nigga?"

"Not a thang homie. Dig this. I'm going to talk fast so catch on even quicker, ya smell me?"

"Yea."

"Do you got a fence to take some ice off my hands?"

"How much ice we talking? And more importantly, how much time we got?"

"Well about three mil in ice, and no time actually. I know I won't get that type of paper, but a mil and a half will be sufficient."

Speaking in his Cuban accent he responded, "Well have you talked to Trick Daddy since he been out? He's got that type of paper on hand. He's really big down here."

"Nah, I haven't. But if you could make the arrangements for

me that would be greatly appreciated. The less people see me, the safer I am."

"I feel ya man. Well look, I'll have that taken care of. I'll do what I can. As far as your ride…"

"Hold up. Don't say no more on these phones. See ya in two hours." Hanging up, he rode in complete silence for the next fifteen minutes thinking about the last week and how all this brought about the demise of his once powerful click. The ringing of his phone brought him out of his deep thoughts. "What it do?"

"It's me baby. I'm at a truck stop in Pekin, Illinois, and those punk bitches are still with me."

"Okay, listen. Here's how we're going to capitalize on their stupidity. I want you to go in and buy a map, find out the directions to Fort Worth, Texas. Take them down that way with you. Also buy another prepaid cell phone while you're there. Leave yours in the women's restroom, let someone else swoop it up."

"Okay. What do I do after I get to Texas?"

"Go to the airport and catch a plane back home. I'll contact you via email. It's too hot for us to meet my love. You're too far along right now to be out here like this. Just go lay back and let me get us a safehouse together okay. Do you trust me?"

"You know I do Daddy."

"Alright. Get rid of that phone. I'm going to lose mine as well. I love you, bye."

With tears streaming down her pretty face, she proceeded to do as he'd instructed, hurt that she couldn't at least see him before having to go back home. Coming this far and not being able to even look at him and see his reassuring eyes was heart wrenching. For a brief moment she had the impulse to somehow lead those punk cops down the highway and cut them off the road. With her impeccable driving skills she was confident she would be able to outsmart them two and run them off down a ravine. But the thought of possibly harming their children in the process or somehow fucking up and getting arrested stopped her, and she did as Dig a Hole instructed. She would never betray him and had already messed up enough as it was.

CHAPTER 49

Letting down the window, he took the phone and threw it into the Mississippi River as he passed it.

Entering Miami brought a little relief to him, but very little. He knew that he could never rest until he was out of America; too much had happened to turn back. Pulling into Little Haiti, a housing complex, he noticed that the police were all over the niggas on the corners. Not wanting to take any unnecessary chances, he drove on to Joe's house.

Pulling up to what looked like a car show, he walked up to the door. Just as he started to knock, Marie, Joe's wife, opened the door. Saying in her sexy Hispanic voice, "Hello. Joe's out back."

"Thank you," was all he said before turning around to head around back. Reaching the backyard, he was greeted by both his old friends Joe and Trick Daddy. Along with Trick Daddy was a cat he introduced by the name of Rick Ross. After the daps and hugs, Dig a Hole got straight to bizness. Seeing a black bag sitting on the hood of the 1972 Caprice, he knew it had money in it. "Dig, let me go get this bag and we can get to business." Coming back with the suitcase he took from Pops, he opened it. Even to his surprise it contained an assortment of jewelry and also two purple Crown Royal bags with uncut stones inside them. Glancing over at Trick he asked, "Are you ready to take this off my hands?"

"Fuck me running. What the fuck, you got Jacob the Jeweler hostage in the trunk, or what?"

"Don't worry, I might."

Thinking silently to himself, Trick figured he probably does have that mutherfucker tied up somewhere. But not giving a fuck about Jacob, or any other jeweler, he just wanted in. "So what ya want for the suitcase?" Trick asked.

"Without the purple bags, 1.5 mil. That's a steal, but you my nigga and I don't feel like wrestling about the price. So I'll show ya love, ya smell me?"

"Dig, that's all good. The only problem is I only got but

$750,000 on the street. Joe, what you got?"

"I got a quarter mil in the crib."

"Well that's a mil partner. Give me til Monday and I'll hit ya with the other half. You know ya boy good, aint I?"

"Alright. We'll let it go like that. But dig, give me your info, numbers and shit because I'll tell ya later how to get it to me. I can't sit still right now."

"I'm already knowing homie." With that, Trick and Ross jumped in the Chevy and departed.

Smiling, Joe asked, "So what you got for me, my friend?"

Without hesitation Dig a Hole tossed him one of the Crown Royal bags of uncut stones. Knowing it was worth at least a million dollars, Joe immediately handed them to his wife and gave Dig a Hole the signal that it was time to move around.

Riding down to the docks, Joe began to explain the arrangement. "I have an uncle who's a General in the Cuban Military, and for the right price he'll give you amnesty. It won't matter who's looking for you, you're safe as long as you stay on Cuban soil. He, along with his chosen men, will meet you personally as soon as you hit Cuban waters. I've arranged for you to be taken there by a good friend of mine who's trustworthy and inconspicuous."

"So what's his price, Joe? What's this going to cost me in total?"

"Well you can give him the diamonds, I'm sure, or a million dollars, which he'll administer out to the right people."

"What about the boat ride?"

"I got that homie. Just take care of General Diaz and you'll be fine."

Pulling up at the docks, they parked Joe's Range Rover and walked up to a boat that appeared to be a speedboat. Not sure that it could safely take him all the way to Cuba, Dig a Hole looked around for another boat, only to find Joe both laughing and walking into the arms of a gorgeous brown-skinned, blond-haired, thick bitch.

"Look homie, this is Goldie. She'll be your driver. And don't let the looks of this boat fool you, this boat is the fastest thing on the water right now. And believe me, you'll need speed."

Still looking at this sexy ass woman in front of him, Dig a Hole tells Joe, "Make sure everything's everything." With a nod of the head, he walks away, leaving the two of them to handle their bizness.

Without as much as a word, Goldie jumped into the boat and smiled at Dig a Hole, revealing two gold teeth, and started checking gauges and other devices on the boat. After ten minutes of this, she fired the boat up, looked over her shoulder and told him, "Buckle up."

CHAPTER 50

Upon arriving at the Fort Worth International Airport, Candyce was still in shock from the reality of the current matter at hand. As if in a trance she slowly made her way to the Northwest Airline ticket booth. As she moved towards the counter, she could have sworn she saw Dig a Hole moving through the crowd, but it was just her heart and mind playing tricks on her.

As she got closer she prayed that by some miracle he would walk up behind her and tell her it was all over and they were going home together. As the ticket agent spoke up saying, "Ma'am, how can I help you? Would you like to purchase a ticket? We have several people behind you in line waiting." she didn't realize that she had been standing in the front of the desk in a daze. It took all the strength she had to purchase a one-way ticket back to St. Paul, Minnesota. As her body started going numb, she walked away.

For the first time thoughts that she may never see Dig a Hole again trickled into her brain. The thought has crossed her mind on several occasions before, but never until tonight had she truly believed it may become a reality. She scrutinized herself for ever allowing those thoughts to enter her mind and cursed today's reality. She then fell nauseous and raced to find a seat, putting one hand over her eyes, and one on her belly.

Here she was, a beautiful, fully pregnant women, crying her eyes out in the middle of an airport in a strange town. After allowing herself a moment, she pulled herself together, not just for herself but for her children and her man.

Pissed that the two idiot agents were still in tow, she decided to take them on a tour of the airport and stopped in a shop to purchase books to read along the way. She didn't know how the hell she would be able to concentrate on reading, but at this point she was liable to drive herself crazy from all this worrying and had to try something. Looking through the racks something finally brought a brief smile to her face. It was just her luck, they had one last copy of Derrick Johnson's newest release, "A Real Goon's Bible". Content with her findings, she made her way to the terminal.

CHAPTER 51

Lying back enjoying the cool ocean breeze, Dig a Hole started to relax. He asked several questions of Goldie but realized she wasn't one to reveal much and cut the conversation short. Noticing a huge, bright light descending upon them he asked, "What the fuck, or shall I say, who is that?"

"Oh shit! Hold on tight. That's the U.S. Coast Guard and we still got about twenty miles to go." Pushing the boat to its fullest potential, the huge Coast Guard boat continued to gain ground and was now being assisted by a helicopter that kept insisting they shut down their engines. Feeling like it was over, Dig a Hole reached inside his bag and cocked his pistol.

"No, don't do that! If you fire on them, they'll blow us out the water. If you don't, we can make it to Cuban waters."

Looking up ahead, Dig a Hole saw about five huge boats lighting up the whole area.

"Yes!" shouted Goldie. "That's what I'm talking about."

Confused as to what was going on, Dig a Hole asked, "What the fuck is that?"

"That baby boy is the Cuban Military. Our escorts."

"Well make me know it. Push this bitch to the limit."

"I gotcha Poppy. Just relax!"

Seeing that there wasn't much else to do but kick back, Dig a Hole watched as the boat he was in entered Cuban waters. Looking back he noticed the Coast Guard back off, along with the helicopter that was on their heels. It gave him a rush like no other sitting back as Goldie guided the smaller boat up alongside a much larger one. He saw a man in military clothing pointing in the direction of the shore as he fired up the boat's engine that would escort them to the mainland.

CHAPTER 52

Relaxing on the white sandy beaches, enjoying the sunset off the Cuban coast, Dig a Hole contemplated his next six moves after receiving word that Candyce had twin baby boys and she and his sister Carla were both in Federal custody for aiding and abetting fugitive flight.

His sons were in his aunt's custody. Seething with anger at how the Feds played his family, he silently made a vow to seek vengeance on any and everyone who had something to do with them being held.

Hearing Goldie's voice brought his mind back into focus. "Baby we have to get ready for my doctor's appointment, as well as pick up your package from the States."

"Yeah okay," kissing her and rubbing their baby in her stomach, he proceeded to head back toward their mini-mansion.

See, after arriving in Cuban waters, the army escorted them to safe grounds. To Dig a Hole's surprise, General Diaz was not just Cuban Joe's uncle, but was Goldie's father, and that was more than he could have asked for. After giving the General the remaining diamonds, the country was opened up to him and Goldie.

As with all things, Dig a Hole's interest was quickly lost; his heart was in the U.S. From time to time they would pop up in Miami for a weekend. Their first trip was to collect the half mil owed to him from Trick Daddy.

While on one of his trips to the States he had a meeting with Joe. That was the beginning of his return. Knowing it would take a lot of preparation, so not to have any poor performances, Dig a Hole returned to Cuba to devise his plan to seek revenge on his enemies and get rich at the expense of others' deaths, by any means necessary.

While lying in a hammock reading "48 Laws of Power" by Robert Green, Dig a Hole's attention was grabbed by the screaming coming from his and Goldie's villa. Jumping up and running towards the villa, he was met at the door by Goldie with a terrified look on her face. "What's the problem baby," questioned Dig a Hole.

"Oh Poppy my water broke. I think it's time to go to the hospital."

Without hesitation he placed her in the car and sped to the nearest hospital. All the way there he was feeling guilty; feeling as if he was betraying Candyce. Knowing in his heart she sat in a Federal jail awaiting sentencing on charges he committed, and not being able to hold her children was more than he believed she could handle. Knowing that she may never get a second chance at life, he knew he'd seek vengeance on every one who had any part of his crew's demise.

The closest hospital was in Havana and as soon as the staff realized who she was they gave her first class royal treatment. She was taken to a ward all to herself with doctors and nurses whose job was to tend to her wants, needs and desires.

Staying by her side trying to comfort her, Dig a Hole couldn't help but feel pain knowing he had twin boys out there who had yet to see their father.

"Oh Poppy it's hurting me, oh shit!" screamed Goldie. Just as Dig a Hole stood to go get help, two doctors and a nurse rushed in. It was only minutes after that he saw his daughter born. Eight pounds and four ounces, big and healthy with a head full of hair. Looking over to Goldie, he saw what appeared to be a glimpse of relief.

The hospital stay was brief. General Diaz had everything arranged for his only child and first grandchild to come home to all the comforts money could afford.

CHAPTER 53

Standing on the patio deck in deep thought, considering when would be the best time to implement his plan, Dig a Hole felt a presence near him. Turning around he stood face-to-face with the General. The General extended his hand toward Dig a Hole and in it was a Cuban cigar. Taking the cigar and biting the tip before lighting it, Dig a Hole turned back around. He knew the General didn't approve of their relationship, but because of Goldie being pregnant he accepted it.

Both of them stood on the deck in complete silence, until the General spoke in his deep voice, "You have made me a very proud man today. And now I welcome you to my family. I've done my research on you and from what I've discovered, you were a petty robber. Well, now I'm going to put you in the big leagues. That's if you're game." With a smirk, he blew a big puff of smoke toward Dig a Hole.

Not knowing if he should feel disrespected by the General's words or happy for what he was offering, even though he didn't know what it was, he turned to the General and started to speak but was cut off before he even got started. The General announced, "7:00 tomorrow morning. Be ready."

With that said he walked off, leaving Dig a Hole at a loss for words: never has anyone spoke or dealt out orders to him. Little did the General know he better watch his ass before he finds himself on the wrong side of Dig a Hole's gun.

At exactly 7:00 am, a black Hummer pulled up outside Dig a Hole's villa. Inside sat a dark-skinned man in army fatigues and mirrored sunglasses with a beret on top of his head. Jumping in the truck, Dig a Hole asked, "Where we going?" It only took seconds to realize the man spoke no English whatsoever.

The ride took a good hour and a half of driving into the mountains, after which they came upon a huge opening with several military men posted up. Stopping the truck next to a grey Jeep, it was then Dig a Hole saw the General smiling while gesturing for him to come over to his vehicle. Climbing into the Jeep, Diaz was the first to speak, "I hope the ride wasn't too long and uncomfortable for you. What I'm about to show you will change your life, this is a fact."

Driving into what appeared to be a dark cave, Dig a Hole had a gut feeling he was being led to his grave. But the thought only lasted a few seconds because inside the cave they came upon a well-built fortress. Pulling the Jeep over about 100 yards inside, they walked into a room that was filled with mounds of cocaine. There was so much cocaine in that room Dig a Hole doubted that it was real. There was literally mountains of it, and all through the room, at least two hundred people went about cutting, weighing and packaging it up.

Turning to look at Dig a Hole, Diaz said, "This is just one room. As you Americans say, I am giving you the key to the city? Well I'm giving you the keys to the country!" With that he laughed a hearty laugh knowing he just blew Dig a Hole's mind.

Trying his best to maintain his composure, Dig a Hole looked toward the General and said, "Yeah this shit here will most definitely give us the advantage we need to cut into the drug trade in the U.S." The General smiled because Dig a Hole said "we". "Keeping it 100% with you, I've never been a drug dealer; at least not on a serious level. I'm a get down or lay down type nigga. Truth be told, I wouldn't know where to start with all this weight."

"Well that, my friend, I will handle. What I need you for is to enforce what we have already established, making sure the bizness is run exactly to my specifications. By doing this you will become one of the richest men in the world, this I promise.

"We've already established ourselves in five major cities – Miami, New York, Chicago, Minneapolis and Detroit. Our objective now is to first rid ourselves of all the competitors in these cities - this is where you come in. If they aint copping from us, then as you say, get down or lay down. Once our dominance is established then we'll branch out, first dominating the entire Midwest. I've taken notice that you have recruited some of our trained assassins. We'll use them to further our agenda."

Shook that the General knew that he had built his little hit squad, Dig a Hole just stood there evaluating all that was being spit at him. Noticing Dig a Hole's surprise that he knew about the female hit squad, the General spoke up saying, "There's not much that goes on that I don't hear or see. I also know you have a female companion and sister as well in Federal holding in Minnesota. They're currently in Sherburne County. Now I may be able to pull some strings to loosen the noose on their necks, but it worries me whether you'll be able to remain focused on the task at hand."

Seeing the seriousness and realizing the power the General had, Dig a Hole's first words were, "If you do whatever you can to help my family, I will be eternally indebted to you. My focus will be solely on dealing with the business at hand. As I'm more than sure you know I'm fully capable of handling this task, so I accept your offer with honor."

Extending his hand, the General pulled him toward him and gave him a fatherly hug, but before releasing him he whispered in his ear, "The price of betrayal is death to everyone you love." Dig a Hole, not one to be intimidated, but by no means anyone's fool, took the comment in stride.

Walking back to the Jeep the General asked, "Are there any questions?" Dig a Hole had only one question, "When do I start?"

"In time son, in time. Things are getting prepared as we speak. It's a must that you become a phantom, due to you being on the F.B.I.'s Most Wanted - Hell you're on the hot sheet with Bin Ladin. So most definitely you will be in and out of everywhere, never sleeping in the same place twice. Goldie will want to accompany you but it is against my wishes. It is up to you to convince her it's best to stay here with LaShyla, no child should be without their mother." His words were like daggers to Dig a Hole's soul, knowing what Candyce was going through.

Instead of it getting him down, Dig a Hole used it as a motivating force to get on top. Yeah he would tend to the General's business, at least until he had the upper hand, then it would be "fuck the General and everything he loves," because Dig a Hole bows down to no man - all the while being smart enough to know to play his position.

Making sure that every detail he planned was precise and on point, choosing to utilize all his new resources to his advantage, Dig a Hole quickly began to assemble his new crew. See Goldie was a very important person in Cuba, because unlike other countries, Cuba has two militaries – one male, one female. Goldie was the head bitch in the female army, giving her the best intel on picking the right people for her and Dig a Hole's private agenda.

After going over hundreds of candidates, they narrowed it down and took sixteen of the most beautiful and dangerous assassins known to man. With Dig a Hole's personal approval Goldie quickly began training the female assassins, getting them prepared mentally as well as physically for what may be their last mission.

Due to all the publicity Dig a Hole received back in the states, it was almost impossible to get a complete grasp on the status of Candyce and Carla. Fortunately he had access to a satellite phone, thus enabling him to make the necessary calls needed to lay down the format to his next plan.

CHAPTER 54

Back in the villa Goldie was working out in the gym. She was not one to just lay around, she was working to get back in shape. The main reason being that she knew Dig a Hole was about to implement his plan and she definitely was not going to be cut out of it. Knowing her father, she knew he was going to put Dig a Hole on and that he wouldn't want her to be a part of it. But little did either of them know they were going to cut her in or cut it out.

Walking into the house, Dig a Hole called out to Goldie. Getting no response he walked to the nursery. Seeing his gorgeous daughter brought a huge smile to his face, but confusion to his heart. Picking his baby up he kissed both her eyes as his Grandmother Eula used to do him. Gazing into her hazel eyes he felt for the first time a sense of real love knowing that LaShyla was his creation. Laying her back in her crib, Dig a Hole left the room in search of Goldie.

Walking into the kitchen he saw her standing in front of the blender making a sport shake. The sun was beaming through the window just right, casting a glow around her golden-colored hair and bronzed-colored skin. Sensing someone's presence, she turned around and smiled because she was deep in thought about him and her father's outing. "Hello handsome. So tell me, was my father's trip a good one or was he being the over bearing person he can at times be?" questioned Goldie.

Her intentions were to simply get him to expose the details of his trip with her father, but wasn't one to be picked for information he wasn't ready to divulge. He responded with a simple reply, "Nah, we just had a man-to-man talk. He's actually just a father concerned about the well-being of his daughter."

Not one to be detoured from her quest, she pushed further. She walked up to Dig a Hole and pulled him close, kissing him passionately while rubbing her hands across his stomach, down into the Sean John shorts he was wearing. Grasping his rock-hard dick in her hand, she seductively looked in his eyes and said, "You need me to handle this for you?"

Casting a downward look at his now exposed ten-inch dick, not waiting for a reply she dropped down to her knees and started from the base of his dick. Licking and sucking her way up to the head of his shaft, feeling the veins pulse from his dick in her hot mouth, she wrapped her sexy lips around him taking in as much as her mouth would allow while rubbing his balls. Looking up at him with her sexy hazel eyes, she moaned.

Looking down at her while she was blowing his brains out, he grabbed her by her long, curly hair and started fucking her mouth, not caring that he was gagging her. He released his load of hot jizzim all down her throat. Not finished, she stood up and pulled him toward the master bedroom. Not wasting any time getting undressed, the two of them embraced.

Kissing her on her soft breasts, he made his way down to her shaven pussy which was dripping wet. Sliding his long hot tongue into her pussy, licking and sucking on her sensitive clit she came fast and fluttered and pulsed around him; her clit shivered against his lips. He lifted himself and told her to turn around. Knowing he liked to fuck her doggy style, she willingly obliged. Smacking her on the ass, he rubbed his fingers in and out her pussy, sliding her pussy juices up to her asshole. He slid his dick into her ass with a vengeful thrust, fucking her like he was a nigga fresh out the pen. He pulled her hair and pounded her asshole while telling her, "Bitch I own you, don't I?"

Feeling his nut about to bust, he pulled out and shot his stream of cum all over her perfectly round ass. Collapsing on the bed, exhausted from the ass fucking, she rolled over and pulled him to her and began to tell him things that she believed he wanted to hear, not knowing his mind and thoughts were elsewhere, thousands of miles away.

CHAPTER 55

Commissioner Jackson of the Minneapolis Police sat behind his huge oak desk looking at his young attractive secretary. After closing the case two years prior on a rogue group of individuals that caused havoc throughout the Twin Cities, he was promoted from Sergeant to Acting Commissioner.

The promotion was right up his alley. Now in control of the department, he had the power to orchestrate the whole program: making it his personal business to go hard on any person or persons that were actively involved in gang activity in the Twin Cities. At times he would go out on late patrols with his Captains and direct raids and sweeps hands-on. After the Bogus

D-Siples shootout on 26ᵗʰ and Colfax, he knew personally the consequences and repercussions behind ignoring the problems that were in the inner city.

It became a known fact that if you were up in Minnesota to hustle, the penalty for getting caught would be severe.

Going over the faxed documents his secretary Crystal handed him, he looked up at her telling her to have a seat. Knowing what he wanted, she nervously took a seat directly across from him. Gazing at her and visually undressing her with his eyes, making her both uncomfortable and scared, he began by telling her he was grateful for her services and then he asked her how long she had been employed with the temp agency that sent her to work for him.

Due to him firing the old, crabby secretary that was there when he was assigned the post, he was in search of his personal assistant, one who not only filed papers and answered phones but one who could bring a little excitement to his boring home life.

"So tell me, do you like working here, Crystal?" Not knowing exactly where he was going with this conversation, she just hoped he wasn't about to fire her - she had two kids to support and couldn't afford to lose a day's work, let alone an undetermined number of days.

Looking him in the eyes she recognized his lustful stare and decided it would be in her best interest to play on it. "Yes, in fact, I enjoy this job immensely. I look forward to coming here everyday, but dread the day my assignment comes to an end."

Knowing he had her, he spoke in a lowered voice, "Look Crystal, I've never been a man to beat around the bush, so let me lay it out for you. I can either hire or fire you. If I'm convinced that you're capable of being a secretary who's willing to go beyond boundaries to keep her boss happy, you've got the job. Ya get the gist of what I'm saying?"

Being a woman who'd been around the block a few times she smiled back at him and said exactly what he wanted to hear, "Not only am I capable, I'm ready and willing to do whatever is deemed necessary to keep my boss happy, both day and night. Now can you feel me?"

"Oh yea I not only feel ya, I want you to come over here and show me you want this job."

Not hesitating she walked around his desk and watched patiently as he pulled his trousers down. Looking at his puny dick she hiked her dress up, pulling her g-string to the side and sat on his dick. Knowing she had some bomb ass pussy she worked it on him, boosting his ego by moaning and telling him how good he made her feel. It was only seconds before he came. Panting and sweating he looked up at her and said, "You're definitely hired!"

Knowing there could never be a better time to make her

demands, she dropped to her knees and started sucking his limp dick. Feeling like he died and went to heaven, he leaned back and closed his eyes. Seeing she had him, she stopped long enough for him to realize she had, and looked him directly in his eyes and said, "I want my salary doubled and a car issued for myself. Daddy, can you make that happen?" She continued to speak in her sweet girly voice all the while massaging his saggy balls knowing he hadn't been treated like this before.

She smiled when he said, "Is that all?"

"For now," she replied while standing up and pulling her dress down. She kissed him on his cheek and turned around and headed back to her office space in the outer room. She stopped at the door, turned around and said, "Call the temp agency and tell them it's a wrap. Their services are no longer needed."

With that she swayed her thick ass out the door. Leaving him in stuck mode.

Sitting there minutes after she left, he stood up, got himself together and proceeded to make some calls. The first being to the temp agency; he most definitely had to keep the young, sexy Crystal satisfied.

CHAPTER 56

Surrounded by manly looking women, Candyce, by choice, stayed to herself. Not familiar with the Federal court system she was virtually being held hostage due to multiple postponements and court dates that were set far apart. After giving birth to two beautiful boys named Galen and Gavin her prison stay seemed unbearable. The worst part being she had no family whatsoever. Dig a Hole was her world. Outside of him she knew nothing else.

It was the not knowing if he was dead or alive that caused the frustration in her to increase. After all the shit hit the fan she saw numerous broadcasts from various news stations talking about a crime spree that started in Minneapolis and went through Chicago, Denver and Kansas. It seemed like they had all the pieces to the puzzle except for the fact that they never claimed to capture or find the remains of her heart and soul. And it was because of this she held on to her faith that if he was alive he would be coming for her one way or another. It just was the when that worried her.

Nevertheless she refused to cooperate with any of the many agents that came to visit her asking questions and wanting answers to things she had no answers to. She now realized just how smart Galen was and how much he really did love her to never involve her in his interactions or provide any information from the streets. It was at times tempting to talk to the agents, especially when they were messing with her about how she may never be apart of her children's lives, or that Dig a Hole was off with KeKe not giving a damn about her or the situation he left her to deal with. But keeping true to him, she never divulged anything at all.

Hearing her name at mail call was surprising to her; she had not once received mail since her incarceration. Walking to the desk to retrieve the mail, she was handed an envelope with no return address but postmarked from Florida. Not sure what it may pertain to she took it inside her cell to read it.

The first line brought instant tears to her eyes because she saw the words *My Dearest Candy Kane*, the nickname Galen called her.

My Dearest Candy Kane,

I'm sorry for all the adversity that you've been through, never would I ever wish this on you. Things have been a little stressful to say the least, but not as stressful as I know you are. Look, an attorney is going to come see you: he's got your best interest at heart. You can trust him. There are things in motion that I can't speak about right now, but some how, some way you will be out to raise those two little boys. Just know out of sight but never out of mind. I need to see you like I need my next breath. I know you're strong so just hold on a little longer, I'm coming for ya. Enclosed is a stack, the lawyer will replace it as you need him to. Take care and don't be letting them dyke hoes lick on my Candy Kane.

Always,

Northside's Finest, the nigga they luv to hate!

After re-reading the letter for the tenth time, Candyce layed on her bunk thinking and planning. Suddenly hope was alive. All of the pain and hurt that she had been through throughout this journey seemed to immediately disappear. Her man was alive and coming for her. She didn't sleep a wink that night as she lay awake going over different scenarios of their first moments together. Soon her family would be together.

CHAPTER 57

Waking up in a cold sweat from the same recurring nightmare was the motivating force Dominique needed to focus on what was really important: the demise of Dig a Hole.

After witnessing the murder of her husband Lord and going through the brutal rape she had to endure, she came out a winner - further proof that it was her right to take over Chicago and to build a team of pure breed niggas that would ride and die for her.

The task at hand wasn't hard to endure due to her taking the two-hundred-eighty bricks of heroin and the mil' ticket cash Lord had stashed in their car outside the hotel. Equipped with all her tools, she formed a tight crew called The Cut Throat Mafia. What started out as a small crew now took over the entire drug game.

Dominique ruled her organization with an iron fist. After twelve years of riding with her husband she had learned the game and wasn't taking no shorts. Since the murder of Lord and the violation of her body, she hadn't been intimate with another man and had become a full-blown dyke.

Calling a meeting of all her top lieutenants, she entered the room looking sexy in her Manolo heels and Gucci blouse and skirt.

"Listen up," drawing the attention of everyone in the room, "I brought ya'll here for the sole purpose of finding out who really wants to get money."

Knowing this would grab everyone's attention, she allowed the comment to manifest in their greedy minds and then continued. "Look, I have a half million dollars cash to the person who brings me this man dead or alive," bending down to a folder on the table, she pulled out a photo of Dig a Hole.

Seeing everyone trying to look at the photo, she continued by saying, "Don't trip. Here, pass it around," she said to Jerome, her closest Lieutenant, handing him the folder.

"Now this is very personal to me. I want him sooner, rather than later. He runs a crew in Minneapolis called the Bogus-D-

Siples. They took a serious hit so they're not as powerful as they once were. There's three grand for every one of them ya'll kill. I want it to be brought to them live and in fucken color. The person who brings me Dig a Hole is guaranteed a half a ticket and their own blocks they currently run."

Looking around at everyone seated in the room, she knew from both the greed in their eyes and their body language that they would go beyond boundaries to cash in on that reward. Little did anyone know she'd give a mil' to get Dig a Hole.

Now confident that they were all on the same page, she continued, "Any info you need is on the back of the photo. By all means don't underestimate any of the muthafuckers. They go hard, which only means we need to go harder. I've had my feelers out for some time now and word is Dig a Hole's M.I.A. But if my husband was correct, he can't and won't stay underground; he's bred to be hands-on, so grab a few of his guys and by choice or not, find out where he is."

Noticing the emotion in her voice everyone couldn't help but wonder why this was so personal. Not that it mattered; hell, everyone in the room had to commit a murder just to be part of the Cut Throat Mafia, so to be paid to clap a nigga was all the incentive they needed.

Speaking up after seeing a break in Dominique's conversation was a cat that went by the name of Slick Pulla. He, by far, was the grimiest person in the room but also the slickest. His conscience went out the door when he found his father molesting his sister and he killed him on the spot at the age of eleven. "Look Baby Doll, this all here sound real sweet, ya feel? Not only will I bring this nigga back for ya, but for the half mil his Momma and Daddy and anyone else that can fit in the trunk. Real talk, I'm up out this bitch headed northbound tonight, so you just go on count that paper up. By the time ya done countin' Slick Pulla will of delivered this nigga to ya, bet that!"

Smiling because she knew he meant every word he said, Dominique finished the meeting by saying, "Like I said. This is personal. This nigga is responsible for killing my husband, so yea I want this one A.S.A.P."

With that being her last words, she left out the room leaving everyone who sat there in deep thought.

StreetLife PUBLISHERS

A REAL GOON'S BIBLE

Destined to be a cult classic

DERRICK JOHNSON

A REALGOONSBIBLE

"All rise! This court is now in session. The Honorable Ronald J. Davis presiding," the Federal Court Deputy yelled at the top of his lungs so that the spectators in the adjacent courtroom could hear.

"Thank you. You may all be seated," said Judge Davis.

"Your Honor, we call Docket Number 008CF256-1, United States vs. Eddie Lee Smith. This matter is on the calendar for sentencing," stated the Court Clerk.

"Thank you, Debbie. State the appearances for the record please," Judge Davis said.

"Your Honor, Attorney Michael Steinley appearing on behalf of the defendant Mr. Eddie Lee Smith, who appears in person. Assistant United States Attorney Richard James Newberry, appearing on behalf of the Government."

"Thank you. Are we ready to proceed with sentencing?" asked Judge Davis. Both parties agreed.

Fast Eddie did a once over of the courtroom. The most important people in his life was present. His newly married wife Fatima, his six year old daughter Jasmine and his eighteen month old son Eddie Jr. His mom and his mistress occupied the other side of the courtroom along with the Channel 4 News correspondent who's been following his case since the day of his arrest, thirteen months earlier. Today was judgment day; the icing on the cake as some would say and Fast Eddie prayed to the heavens above that his mom and wife would get along. Momma Smith, as the hood knew her, never approved of Fatima. She always felt that Fatima was a gold digger who trapped her son with two unwanted kids. But out of the love for her son, she kept her distance and her thoughts to herself. But Fatima knew how she felt.

Two U.S. Marshals were at the exit doors of the courtroom, "Fags," Fast Eddie thought to himself. They toted .45 caliber, semi-automatics which was standard Government Issue now-a-days. Neither probably ever discharged their weapons in the line of duty, but wouldn't think twice if the opportunity ever arose.

A tap on Fast Eddie's leg from his attorney brought him back to reality and the matter at hand. "Your Honor", the AUSA started, "I would like to address an issue I have regarding an email I received from Mr. Steinley late yesterday afternoon in respect to Defendant Smith."

"Okay, go ahead," Judge Davis said as he bent his head down and looked over the top of his glasses as your third grade teacher would have done. Throughout the course of this case there has been constant back and forth bickering between the Assistant United States Attorney and the Defendant's Attorney. Judge Davis wasn't about to allow this hearing to turn into one of the previous ones.

"Mr. Steinley went into great detail, which I would like to share with you," Mr. Newberry said as he proceeded to the Judge's bench to give him copies of the email that the

Defendant's Attorney sent him. "As you can see, Mr. Steinley pointed out how Count One of the Four-Count Indictment, 21 U.S.C. 846 Conspiracy should be dismissed based solely on the fact that the defendant has no co-defendants."

"Well I'm unsure if now is the right time to address this issue," interrupted Judge Davis. "This is a matter that should have been addressed prior to sentencing. This court doesn't have the authority to dismiss a jury's finding. Today is solely for sentencing purposes, not the finding of guilt or innocence which was determined at trial. Therefore, I will not allow the discussion of whether or not conspiracy is appropriate. However, I will add for the purpose of the record under U.S. Title 21, Subdivision 846, it states in part, conspiracy involves an agreement by two or more people to commit an unlawful act. It goes on further to state that the co-conspirators can be a person or persons known to the Court, indicted and unindicted," finished Judge Davis.

Fast Eddie turned around and looked at his mother who looked as if she had no clue as to what was going on. All she knew was that the white man was trying to send her son to prison for a long time. Momma Smith grew up in the "Jim Crow Days.", a time when there was Black Unity and Black Power; also where a time when blacks rebelled against the white man and the system instead of each other. And even to this very day the whitey is still a suspect to her.

Fatima had just come back in the courtroom from changing Eddie Jr.'s diaper and caught the tail end of the Judge's statement. She blew Fast Eddie a kiss and moved her lips as to say, "I love you." That kinda eased his mood a bit. It is amazing how something so simple from a woman could change a man's mood from bad to good.

"Thank you, Your Honor," Mr. Newberry said and Judge Davis instructed him to proceed. "Your Honor, this case is one that has bothered me since it was first assigned to me for a number of reasons. One was the amount of the drug that was involved, two was the type of drug that Mr. Smith possessed, and three there were guns involved in this case. In addition, the defendant's lack of responsibility is a concern. He has shown absolutely no remorse throughout any of his court proceedings. Your Honor, Mr. Smith has been convicted of possessing over seven kilograms of cocaine with at least five hundred grams of it being crack cocaine and various firearms violations. Unfortunately we all know the harm drugs and guns can do to a community and its families. Needless to say, any penalty that calls for 262-327 months in prison is serious, serious stuff. Mr. Smith's Pre-Sentence Investigation Report shows that he has been involved in not only the criminal life, but also the criminal justice system since the age of twelve. That's more than half of his life! I recall during one of the hearings his attorney said, "My client is not a bad person." While I believe that Mr. Steinley was sincere in his belief that his client was not a bad person, nevertheless words are relative. What may be not so bad to him, may be horrible to me, and vice versa. Mr. Smith has ties to the 2-4 Organization."

"I object, Your Honor. There is no evidence to substantiate that," said Attorney Steinley as he rose from his seat. "My client hasn't been convicted of being a part of any organization."

"Sustained," Judge David said. "Strike it from the record. Let's stick with the facts here Mr. Newberry."

"Okay, Your Honor. If we'll be honest here for a minute, Mr. Smith has become the exceptional criminal and I believe that the Criminal Justice System has allowed him to get to this point. As I looked over his PSI I noticed how Mr. Smith has been arrested time and time again for various crimes, only to be released and rearrested and released again. Mr. Smith has been incarcerated for a total of sixteen months throughout his life of crime, and my belief is had the message gotten to him sooner, that his behavior is highly unacceptable and will not be tolerated in our society, we may not be here today. We also have to look at the disparity in the communities. What's going on here in Milwaukee I'm sure will not have any affect on the drug trade in Chicago, Los Angeles, St. Louis or any other place for that matter. But we have to take a stand and send a message to Mr. Smith that we don't want his kind here. Your Honor we need to keep his kind out so that we don't become like the other cities, for lack of a better phrase. Therefore, I strongly believe that Mr. Smith is a prime candidate for every last one of the 327 months he is facing. Thank you, Your Honor."

As the Assistant U.S. Attorney headed back to his seat he nodded at Fast Eddie as if to say, "I got you." Fast Eddie showed no facial expression. His motto is and has always been, "Never let them see you sweat." He knew there was an art to playing the cards you were dealt, and he did it well.

Street Life
P U B L I S H E R S

P.O. Box 2112
Minneapolis, MN 55402
www.streetlifepublisherz.com

Available Now!

Get Down Or Lay Down By Derrick Johnson	**$15.00**
A Real Goon's Bible By Derrick Johnson	**$15.00**
Cut Throat Mafia By Derrick Johnson	**$15.00**
Murda Squad By Derrick Johnson	**$15.00**
Street Kingz By Derrick Johnson	**$15.00**
Crooked By Anthony Creach	**$15.00**
Supply And Demand By Javetta Taplette & Derrick Johnson	**$15.00**
Omerta By Larry Eat'em Up Brown	**$15.00**
Jealousy Breeds Envy By Robert Williams	**$15.00**
Jackerz By Cool Daddy Swag	**$15.00**

Coming Soon! 2015

Lay It Down By Derrick Johnson (Sequel To Get Down Or Lay Down)

Dangerous Minds By Wakinyan Wakan Mcarthur

Turned Out By Edward Robinson

Shattered But Not Broken By Lakesha Johnson

Jealousy Breeds Envy Trilogy By Robert Williams

Love Me Not A Collection Of Nightmares By Larie Lewis

(Shipping and handling is $3.99 for 1st book and $1.99 for each additional book. Acceptable forms of payment are money order or instituional checks ONLY. *All books are $13.99 for institutions.* FOR ONLINE PURCHASES LOG ONTO WWW. STREETLIFEPUBLISHERZ.COM. All orders are shipped within 36 hours from the time they reach the office and are sent confirmation delivery. If you need the status of your order, please email customer service at Derrick@streetlifepublisherz.com.

TOTAL $ _____

Purchaser Information

Name: _____

Reg. # _____

Address: _____

_____

_____

City: _____

State: _____   Zip: _____

Total number of books ordered: _____

39372570R00137

Made in the USA
Middletown, DE
20 January 2017